THE HAUNT

As you'd expect of the Ma[...] Scott has always been fascinated by ghosts and the supernatural. "I like spooky things," he says. "I grew up reading ghost stories, listening to them on the radio and I've had some creepy experiences of my own." It's no wonder then that he writes spine-chilling stories himself.

It was in 1984, two years after winning the Woman's Realm Children's Story Writing Competition that he decided to give up his job as an art teacher and become a full-time writer: "I had this feeling inside me, just sitting in my solar plexus – a little diamond of pure knowledge, very hard and strong, and I knew it wouldn't go away until I left teaching and became a writer." His first novel, *The Shaman's Stone*, was published in 1988 and several more titles soon followed. These include *Why Weeps the Brogan?* (Winner of the 1989 Whitbread Children's Novel Award), *Something Watching*, *The Gargoyle*, *A Box of Tricks*, *The Place Between*, *The Camera Obscura*, *Freddie and the Enormouse* and, most recently, *The Ghosts of Ravens Crag*.

Hugh Scott is married with two grown-up children and grandchildren and lives in Scotland.

Other books by Hugh Scott

For younger readers

Freddie and the Enormouse
The Summertime Santa

For older readers

A Box of Tricks
The Camera Obscura
The Gargoyle
A Ghost Waiting
The Place Between
The Shaman's Stone
Something Watching
Why Weeps the Brogan?

THE HAUNTED SAND

HUGH SCOTT

WALKER BOOKS
AND SUBSIDIARIES
LONDON • BOSTON • SYDNEY

First published 1990 by Walker Books Ltd
87 Vauxhall Walk, London SE11 5HJ

This edition published 1996

2 4 6 8 10 9 7 5 3 1

Text © 1990 Hugh Scott
Cover illustration © 1996 Bruce Pennington

Printed in Great Britain

British Library Cataloguing in Publication Data
A catalogue record for this book is available
from the British Library.

ISBN 0-7445-5216-8

For
MY MOTHER
with love

Chapter 1

Norfolk. Tuesday morning.

Frisby Allen fled among the trees.

"Oh, Mummy!" she gasped.

Rain rattled on full-grown summer leaves. The trees leaned, black with water. Frisby's wellingtons struck hard at mud splash! splashing! as she ran, as she glanced back.

Her foot leaped sideways, smacking Frisby's short height flat on the path, and the mud's cold cheek met her face, its brown taste on her tongue.

She squealed. She spat. And rose stickily, staring among the dark morning branches, striving to see past quivering leaves; she touched the mud on her good red coat; rain found ways among her curls, and laid chill trickles on her scalp. Air in her mouth sped fresh with vegetable smells. She listened.

She tightened her mouth against tears, then snarled, knowing her white teeth shone in her brown face.

A growl rumbled in her throat and hair bristled on her neck. She said, "George?" and stared at the moving woods.

Then a sound – not rain hammering, not the wind – sent blood surging coldly under her skin.

Metal creaked.

She ran again, swiftly, feet firm at each stride, arms up to fend off slapping leaves, towards the low turquoise sky and the fence that stretched between her and the meadow.

She ducked through the fence's wires and raced over grass that bent beneath the rushing air. She stopped.

She looked back; only the grass moved, and the trees gathered, wild-armed beneath boiling clouds.

Then she ran down the long slope to the house; rubber feet booming on the metal bridge; reeds struggling in the river pretending they were drowning.

Fear left Frisby as her feet ceased booming and crunched on gravel, splashed in mud among the red brick walls of the stable, the Small Barn and the back of the house.

Her coat swung wet around her knees. Her curls hung with mud. She felt her knee push through a hole in her tights. She opened the back door and stood on the step trying not to cry like a little girl.

Chapter 2

Mother.

Warm air, moist with the smell of soup, engulfed Frisby, and Mother glanced up with a smile, glanced again, gaping. "Frisby?" Dropped the knife among green tufts of parsley.

"Frisby!"

"Mum!"

"In!" shrieked Mother. "Close the door!"

"I *fell!*"

"Look at you! Don't move! You've been running! You're not twelve any longer! Can't you walk!"

"It's George's fault! He scared me! He dared me to go to the haunted church! He chased me!"

"Coat off! That isn't true! Boots! Look at your tights! These are for the bin —"

"My socks are dry."

"Don't change the subject! You can't blame George for everything! I know he teases you. I know he's worse when his father's away – how am I going to clean this coat?"

"George —"

"George came home on his bike five minutes ago, so whoever chased you it wasn't —"

Mother, holding the coat by the scruff of its neck, stared down. Frisby saw her anger fade. "Did someone really chase you?"

Frisby's throat filled with tears. She nodded.

She stepped out of her skirt; hauled off her jumper.

"Sure?"

Nod.

"Shower. Even your underwear's wet. Watch you don't meet Darren on the stairs. George brought him home. Someone from the school?"

"What?"

"Chasing you. For a joke."

"Maybe."

Mother sighed, and Frisby, brown legs and arms bare, left footprints on the tiles.

"The haunted church!" said Mummy, and Frisby closed the door.

She shivered, her neck and shoulders wet, trickles from her hair running on her back and under her bra. Sometimes she hated George! But she couldn't shout at him dressed like this, and creepy Darren was the last boy on earth she'd want to meet.

She hurried upstairs, silently past George's door and the drone of Darren's voice; into the bathroom, under the shower, mud from her hair running on her brown skin. She thought how fair George was; and his father. Fair and handsome. George senior, handsome as a film star. Frisby always thought of him in a grey topper and tails, with Mother beside him in a cream wedding dress that showed off her coffee-soft complexion; and herself, two years smaller, neat-footed, clasping a lilac posy, and George, nearly Mother's height, tense at his father's arm.

That was the first time she'd met Darren. She

still didn't like him. Frisby rubbed a second lather of shampoo into her curls. She didn't like his voice, as dull as television too loud in the next room, and she did not like – Frisby straightened under the shower stretching her back – she did not like the way he spoke, as if secrets lay behind ordinary events and only he knew what these secrets were. "Smirking brat!" she said aloud and spluttered shampoo.

The warm rain of the shower returned her to the church. George daring her to go. "Not scared of spooks, Frizzy!" Frisby wishing she wasn't wearing her coat. Though why she shouldn't on such a dull morning... It was nice to feel good. Pity about the wellies.

She had needed the wellingtons, though, following George and Darren on the beach. And she had taken the dare, holding her coat away from the hedgerow as she strode in the oat field, George's braying faint among the dunes behind her. She knew he'd follow.

To her right, the windmill had groaned through its arm exercises.

Then rain tapped leaves as she trod into the wood. She knew George was coming – and Darren. Though she hadn't seen either.

She stood beside blocks of stone, crisp in ivy jackets. She shivered as the rain settled down to soaking her hair. Among the trees rose just one wall of the church; a threatening bulk of dark flint, with a doorway too full of nettles, too soft with shadow, to dare approach.

The chill increased as rain drummed the

11

ground; as if someone had switched off summer. Then the wind leaned on Frisby, carrying George's voice, still in the oat field. And Frisby said, "George?" hopefully to a gap in the trees. "Darren!" in a shriek. "Is that you!"

She heard feet running, but light feet, like a child's; and a man raging; and a ringing scream so distant it must have been a dream.

Frisby walked on. The path melted into mud. Let them try to scare me! She turned up her collar.

She would go home, and wait with dignity, pretending she hadn't heard their teasing. George was a beast.

She hadn't thought Darren would join in such a prank. Creep.

The wind rushed up behind her.

Metal jangled.

She began to run, holding her coat close.

She looked back and saw a million leaves waving.

She ran faster.

On the path beside her, arose a sound of weeping.

Chapter 3

Darren.

Frisby shrieked as the shower ran cold. She turned it off, squeezed her hair partly dry, bound a towel into a turban, and wore the bath towel like a gown.

She peered onto the landing. George's voice rose, excited, above Darren's monotone. She darted to her room and put a chair against the door. She didn't want George bursting in – especially with Darren on tow. Ugh!

From the north window, Frisby gazed onto the red-brick stables and Small Barn. She loved the soft-red ripple of the tiles, and their dapples of moss. She enjoyed watching the thrust of the river as it pushed beneath the little iron bridge. Beyond the bridge the earthen path faded up to the top of the hill. Not that it was much of a hill. But it hid the wood. She was glad of that. Had she really been chased?

She stepped into tan cord trousers and burrowed inside a winter jumper. What a rotten day for August! This morning had turned just a bit dull and a good excuse to dress up, but the chill that had come with the rain, lingered.

"I hope it warms up for the rest of the holidays!"

She tugged an Afro comb through her hair, then dashed to the stairs, but stopped, wondering at George's voice still braying excitedly through the shut door.

Curiosity tilted Frisby's head. She couldn't make out George's words. She stood close to the door, pushing dust along the rim of a panel with her little finger. "Haunted!" bellowed George.

Frisby turned the handle and pushed. The door jammed, and Frisby pulled. She kicked away a sock with her slippered toe.

"Who wants to touch that!" she said.

"Here it comes," groaned George, but his glance was friendly.

"What's haunted?" asked Frisby. "The church?"

"Nothing."

"The shore. At Longman's Reach." Darren held something under his hand. His eyes glittered green, wrinkled around like an old man's, and his mouth tightened to one side.

"What have you got?"

"It's…" Darren's gaze slid towards George. "Shall we tell?"

"You and your secrets!" said Frisby. "It's a bit of metal."

"Promise not to tell?"

"She's all right," said George.

"Gee, thanks," said Frisby and glanced up at God.

Darren's fingers splayed flat. On his palm was balanced a strip of metal, like a narrow bookmark, green as his eyes, spreading wide at one end, rotted along its edges.

"Fascinating secret," sighed Frisby. "What's it

got to do with the beach being haunted?"

"Look at it closely," said George.

Frisby lifted the metal. "Ooh! It's a bit horrid. Cold. There's a hole in the wide end. Why is it green?"

She wiggled her pinkie through the hole and found door-dust still on the tip. She dropped the metal into Darren's hands and wiped her finger on her trousers.

"It's bronze," croaked Darren. He laid the metal on his nose, the wide end spreading above his eyes, and for a moment the green glitter of wet retinas and the green grime of the metal made a demon's mask full of power and wickedness.

Frisby stepped back. George said "Come on!" in a little gasp, and Darren's palms spread, skin thin as tissue-paper, and wrinkled.

Frisby peered at his hands, but Darren dropped the metal into them and folded them away.

"Bronze?" said Frisby.

"Thirteen forty-nine," said Darren.

"Come on!"

"How can you know that! Nobody knows the date! It's only scrap!"

"You saw that it's part of a helmet. Thirteen forty-nine! I know! The hole took a rivet fastening it to leather! Bronze and leather! Bones and leather —"

"What's he saying!" Frisby stepped beside George.

"He goes a bit funny at times," breathed George. "Take it easy, Darren."

"The beach is haunted." Darren's hair stood

rough-tufted like a wet cat. "I found it on the beach —" His glance slipped over Frisby. " — while you went across the oat field to the old church."

"Huh!" said George.

"You were shouting after her. I picked this up." He touched the metal, and bent to the floor, curl-backed over his discarded anorak, searching a pocket. Things clicked. Something black escaped his fingers and bounced on the carpet. It seemed to Frisby that Darren thrust another object into the depths of the anorak. But perhaps not.

George lifted the dark thing. "A chicken bone," he announced. "An exciting find for our mad archaeologist!"

"It's human," said Darren. He turned his left hand palm down, took the bone, and laid it along the back of his finger. "Shorter than mine, but a phalanx. Definitely."

"Why is it black?" whispered Frisby.

"Why is the helmet green? Y'know, I found the helmet between the dunes, the smallest corner peeping —"

"Was that all of it?" asked George. "No more bits?"

"More?" said Darren. His fingers hid the bone, like a conjurer about to perform magic. His mouth pulled up into its bent smile, but his glance lowered.

"I didn't look for more. Rain. You remember, George? Wasn't the rain cold? I heard you calling after Frisby. The sand was orange. And harvestmen dashed into their holes. Then the wind rushed off the sea…" Darren's eyes touched Frisby. "I felt someone watching me. I heard —"

"Not guilty!" from George.

"I had to get out of there. I called George back."

"You mean you didn't follow me!" gasped Frisby.

"Why should we follow a little brown bear?" asked George.

"You didn't follow me across the oat field?" Frisby was startled to see the bone again, on the back of Darren's hand. "*Was* someone watching you?" she asked.

Darren shrugged.

"It looks like a chicken bone to me!" said Frisby.

"It was with the helmet," murmured Darren.

"*You* say it's part of a helmet! It could be any old thing! *You* say the bone is human!" Fear raised Frisby's voice, because if George hadn't followed her…

"You're forgetting who my father is," smirked Darren.

"Just because he's a doctor it doesn't mean you know all about bones!"

"The skeleton?" sighed Darren. "From his student days? In his study? I have drawn every bone. I *know* this is human."

Frisby said, "Hmn," between firm lips. She knew Darren's drawings. Lines like wire, and out of proportion.

"I don't believe it," she persisted. "Are you saying somebody's buried there? Or washed up?

Where's the rest of him?"

"I don't know yet."

"We're going to look," said George, and Darren slid a glance that reddened George's face. "It's not a secret," mumbled George.

"Everything's a secret with Darren!" snapped Frisby.

"I was about to tell you…"

George moved away, as if he didn't care.

"What?" demanded Frisby. She was bored with Darren's mysteries. A chicken bone, a scrap of metal, and a cold breeze. *That* was his secret.

"I heard something."

"I didn't," said George.

"The wind," said Frisby. "Coots —"

"I know the sound of wind in the dunes. I know the sound of coots. I heard a child running —"

"*What?*"

" — and a man shouting. I heard a woman screaming, far away, and yet close around me in the sand. And weeping! Weeping, Frisby! Weeping for something done that couldn't be undone! Murder, Frisby! Murder on the beach!"

Chapter 4

Ghosts.

"Murder!" yelled George, looming over Frisby.

"Don't be stupid!" howled Frisby. "Stop waving your arms in my face! How does he know? How does he know anything? I don't believe you!"

Frisby fled, slamming the door so the house shook, heavy-footed on the stairs, seething, "Creep! Creep!" Finding Mother in the kitchen round-eyed with anger; the coat's liquid front caking dry at an electric radiator; boots steaming, the smell of rubber spoiling the smell of soup.

"Sorry, Mummy. But that Darren!"

Mother spent a grim few seconds wiping the kitchen table. Frisby felt she was in school again; in trouble again. Mother's school-teacher past gave authority to every move of her hands, the turn of her curly head, the flat-backed poise as she gazed down on Frisby. "Sit," said Mother, and Frisby sat. The blocks of wood of the butcher's table showed square patterns of grain, slightly moist from Mother's cloth, drying rapidly from the edges inward.

Mother spoke quietly. "Did someone chase you?"

"I thought so. I wouldn't have run —"

"Wouldn't you?"

"I wouldn't! Not in my coat! Not through the

mud! There was something there! Darren heard it! He says the beach is haunted!"

"Darren was here with George." Mother sighed and went to the kettle.

"He heard it! They ran away from Longman's Reach!"

Mother put cups on the table and tipped in milk. "Shall I get Darren down here, and ask him?"

"If you like." Then Frisby realized Mother was challenging her honesty. "I don't want tea, thank you."

Mother bumped the milk bottle onto the table. Frisby stared proudly, and saw doubt in her mother's eyes.

"I don't lie," she whispered.

"Hmn," said Mother, and Frisby relaxed as the kettle boiled. "Will my coat be all right?"

Mother poured the tea and rested the pot on the table.

"Longman's Reach," she said.

Frisby waited. "Any biscuits?"

"Tin."

Frisby put the tin beside the cups. "What about Longman's Reach?"

"I'm trying to remember something." Mother's pretty face turned seriously on Frisby. "But I want to know, definitely, if someone chased you. If there's some lunatic —"

Frisby was shaking her head.

"No one chased you?"

"I don't mean that, Mum. I mean..." Frisby sighed. "I don't think it was a person —"

"An animal? There's nothing around here —"

"No! Not an animal. Oh, I don't know! A ghost! Ghosts! Ghosts in the wood! A child running! A man shouting!"

Mother's hand clenched on Frisby's fingers. "A woman screaming —"

"Yes!"

Mother's eyes widened into brown circles. Her fingers pressed Frisby's bones painfully. "But I can't remember where I heard it —"

"Oh, Mum!"

" – or read it. Or what it's supposed to mean. If anything. Oh, I'm sure it portends something awful."

"Darren said murder."

"I don't think it was murder. Though you were nearly murdered when you came in with your coat…" Mother drank her tea. "I expect I'll remember in the bath, or during the night, when there's nobody to tell."

"Your George will be home tomorrow."

"Yes." Mother smiled. Her gaze drifted around the kitchen and Frisby knew she was thinking about her husband; seeing through the kitchen walls with their tall cupboards, to the other rooms, quaintly grand, and the views north, of curved fields; and to the front, houses built this century, red brick and flat gardens.

"You do like him?" Mother's eyes warmed suddenly on Frisby.

"It's been two years!" said Frisby.

"But you do?"

"You know I do. And you love him a lot, don't

you?"

Mother nodded.

"Better than Daddy?"

"Better?" sighed Mother. "That's not a question you should ask. There's no real answer. Different. But, oh, so good! We change, Frisby. Our attitudes change. We go on growing up; all our lives, if we want. The past is gone. We must forgive ourselves for mistakes. Forgive other people. Live now! I love my George and I love you. I love young George and this place. Are there old scores to be settled? Forgive, Frisby, and old scores just die, because they don't matter."

Mother sighed again, and left her cup on the table. She lifted the soup pot lid and put her face in the steam. She stirred deep with a wooden spoon.

"Do you believe in ghosts?" asked Frisby.

"I don't think so. I'll turn the soup off. We'll have it later."

"Creepy Darren's not staying for lunch is he?"

"If he wants."

"Oh, Mum!"

"Weren't you asking a serious question?" Mother sat down and topped hot tea into her cup. "Tell me again what you heard in the wood."

And Frisby spoke while Mother nuzzled her cup; smiled; laughed a little. "It sounds to me like ghosts! Though," she added quickly, "I expect it was the wind. Branches. A crisp bag blowing along."

"George being an idiot," said Frisby hopefully.

"He was here. Oh, I don't suppose it was anything…"

"Then how did you know about the screaming? And Darren did say he heard it on the beach. He did. While George was shouting after me. While I was still in the oat field."

"If that's so…"

"It's what he said."

"I believe you. But if that's so, then he heard it before you did. How odd." Mother's curly head bent as if listening to her own thoughts. A smile brought her teeth glinting with excitement.

"What?" whispered Frisby. "What is it?"

"Well if Darren heard it on the beach, then a little later you heard it —"

"At the church."

"Yes. Well don't you think that maybe…"

"Yes?"

"Maybe our ghosts *started* from the beach —"

"Started?"

"Started from the beach," said Mother. "Started from the beach, and ran in their ghostly nightshirts, all the way to the wood?"

Chapter 5

Psychometry.

Silence stood in the kitchen.

Dried mud dropped from Frisby's coat and clicked on the tiles. Wind dashed rain against the window.

"It's an idea," said Frisby.

Not a nice idea. Somehow, Mother-not-believing was better than Mother-believing.

"You don't mean it, Mum."

"England is full of ghosts." She stood up gathering the teacups. "I hear phantom footsteps."

The footsteps battered closer and the door opened. "Any grub!" cried George. "Darren can stay to lunch, yes? Say yes, Angel!"

"Yes!" said Mother. "Stop kissing the top of my head! I know you're bigger than me. But I'm still the boss. Are you hungry or excessively hungry?"

"Starving!"

"That mean's just hungry. Go away for ten minutes. Come back clean."

"Whoo!" yelled George at Frisby as he passed. "Seen any spooks!" His feet clattered up the stairs.

"Pig! Pig!" yelled Frisby. "Smelly pig," she muttered, then heard herself, and giggled.

"I'll do them chips," said Mother. "Do you

want —?"

"No thanks, Mum. I'm off animal fat."

"It's vegetable oil."

"I'll make a sandwich. I wonder if there's a tomato ready."

"Well, don't fall going to the greenhouse."

"Mum!" said Frisby. "Oh, this weather! How can August be so wet! According to T.P. Appleman —"

"Who's T.P. Appleman?"

"He wrote our geography book. T.P. Appleman says Norfolk is the driest part of the country. And I need my anorak just to cross the yard!"

Frisby ran to the cupboard under the stairs. She stepped into wellingtons, and decided she would wear Mother's plastic raincoat. She realized, standing in the hall with rain rushing against the front door, and cold plastic buttoned under her chin, that she was scared. Mother's coat around her was a comfort; comfort that protected her down to the ankles of her red wellies.

George and Darren thudded from the bedroom, stairs trembling at their descent. George leaned over the banister. "Watch out for spooks in the coat cupboard!"

"You're the only spook around here!"

Frisby frowned at their backs, George, tall, with good shoulders, Darren short and broad but curved as if hiding too many secrets. "Darren!" said Frisby.

"Oops! Find a ghost?" cried George.

Darren smiled.

"What made you think," asked Frisby lightly, "that the helmet was thirteen forty-nine? I mean, the date wasn't stamped on it."

"Made in Hong Kong!" brayed George.

"Well." Darren moved towards her, walking slightly sideways, eyelids exposing his eyes a flicker at a time. He stood beyond her reach. "Well," he said again.

"Hurry up!" said George. "I smell chips. Any ham, Angel?" George vanished into the kitchen, the door easing shut behind him, pressing shadows into the hall.

Darren said, "Huh!" in a little laugh, and a wrinkled palm turned towards Frisby. "I don't tell anyone. People. You know. They think things. I don't care about cricket, you see. I wonder if you understand. George does, in a way."

"What's cricket got to do with it? No, I don't understand —"

"Listen. Listen. It's being normal. Liking cricket, football. Thinking about girls. You know. Oh, I like girls well enough, but history and mathematics organized until the life is squeezed out of them. I'm not explaining very well." Darren gazed at Frisby's wellingtons.

"You're not explaining at all," she said firmly.

"No." His eyes flickered green. He didn't come any closer. "I'm interested in other things!" Enthusiasm leapt in his voice, but the words fled quietly through the hall.

"I love old objects. I love to feel the past in my palm. I *know* that a man wore that helmet six and a half centuries ago!"

"I can understand —"

"The metal speaks to me! It speaks to *me*, Darren Wycroft. No one understands. Not even George. But George believes. I don't have any other friends. Perhaps you."

Frisby shrank inside Mother's coat. "You haven't really told me —"

Darren stepped closer, and Frisby's neck tensed, but she managed not to retreat. "You think," whispered Darren, "that I pretend to have secrets, and you are right. Because someone who has real secrets gets the habit of not telling. Oh, I'm not a criminal, Frisby. I'm not weird. I'm not even a creep —"

Frisby felt guilty.

" – but I do have secrets, simply because no one can understand. Do you know what psychometry is?"

Frisby's head shook, the coat, warm now, under her chin, the cuffs chill lines across her hands.

"Thirteen forty-nine," breathed Darren. "That scrap of metal, as you called it – that scrap, when I saw it, called on me to pull it from the sand. My fingers knew it was a helmet. They could ... there is no word! Taste. My fingers could taste the leather that was no longer there! And when I held it, I felt its whole shape, and knew the living head it encased. I knew the sword stroke that ended the terror of its owner. The greed in his soul; the cold damp of a summer long ago, and death in every breath of air."

Darren stood panting.

27

A pulse beat in Frisby's temple and she rubbed the side of her head.

Darren sighed loudly. "You won't tell anyone?"

"No. I have to go out now." She moved round him, and he turned to keep facing her.

"No one understands."

"*I* don't understand," muttered Frisby. His eyes shot green. "But I won't tell." She ran out the front door.

She should have gone through the kitchen, but the front was the quickest way to fresh air.

"Oh!" she cried, and breathed deeply. Rain swung across the doorstep. "Oh, golly!" she yelled and went into the rain, face up to the raindrops; remembering mud in her mouth.

Mother's roses turned their bonnets from the wind. Hollyhocks swung on trellises against the ancient brick beside the door. And round about, this century's homes sat in their generous gardens, with fields beyond, stunning yellow, wild with their second crop of oilseed rape.

Frisby ran round the house, and across the yard to the greenhouse built against the stable wall, paint flaking from its wooden bones, putty cracked. George had meant to replace the putty this summer. But then, he had meant to do it last summer. Frisby was glad she would see him tomorrow.

She closed the greenhouse door. Rain blurred the glass. She shivered. Darren really had given her the creeps.

Tomato plants stood green-handed against the

back wall, the red wall of the stables; the wall, Frisby noticed yet again, that rose from the ground as dark stone, because the brick was built on old foundations.

She wondered if the stones had been part of stables in thirteen forty-nine. Or someone's house. Why, she could be standing now where the man with the helmet ate his breakfast. Frisby felt chilled. The greenhouse shouldn't be as cold as this.

She searched for ripe tomatoes. Sometimes a tiny red baby beamed among the greenery. Frisby lifted a leaf. Plenty of fruit, but hard as apples.

Ah. A sparkle of red touched her eye. She walked up the centre of the greenhouse.

Cucumbers hanging, strangely disturbing.

A wasp vibrated under the glass roof.

She eased aside a leaf, pressed the tomato's softness, and lifted it free of its stalk.

She shivered.

A small sound found her ear and she turned.

Between her and the door stood a child.

Frisby's hand crushed the tomato to death, its blood cold between her fingers.

Screams soared out of her.

Chapter 6

Tuesday afternoon.

Screaming filled her mind.

Screaming used the energy pumped by her heart into her limbs. She saw the wasp descend the slant of the roof and drop to the small green world of a tomato.

She saw, through blurred glass, the kitchen doorway darken as the door opened inwards. A figure hesitated, then ran.

Frisby's screams trembled on every pane.

Mother rushed open-armed up the length of the greenhouse engulfing Frisby in warmth and the smell of chips.

"Stop! Oh, stop! What is it? Frisby!"

But Frisby screamed on, keeping her mind from the child.

Then her throat closed, releasing only terrible groans; and tears rose inside her face and fled from her eyes. Then Mother and George, with Darren behind them, led Frisby to the kitchen, on to a chair; Mother comforting, urging George to make tea, questioning gently, asking over and over if she was hurt.

"Oh, Mum! A little girl! A little girl!" Frisby heard the words repeated from her own mouth.

She heard Darren whisper that his father was home; and Darren left. Then he returned, and Dr Wycroft asked quiet questions which Frisby found breath to answer. She lay in bed, merest touches of the doctor's fingers around her face and neck. Murmurs of reassurance.

Tea, sweet as toffee.

"Let her sleep for an hour or two, Mrs Gray. Let me know if there's any change."

"Oh, Mum!" Frisby collapsed back from her soup plate. "Thanks, Mum. There wasn't any meat in that?"

"No, but there's meat in this. I thought steak pie, after your fright."

Gravy oozed from under golden flakes of pastry.

"Come on!" said George. "If you don't want it —"

"Oh, be quiet! I had no lunch." Frisby delved into the pie.

"Darren was very good," said Mother.

"Yes," said Frisby.

"He examined the greenhouse. He's really quite clever —"

"Very clever!" cried George.

"Pointed out the prints of your wellingtons and my slippers —"

"And my shoes. I came to your rescue too, you know. Said you'd see a spook, didn't I?"

"Shut up," mumbled Frisby around a mouthful of pie.

"He didn't find any other foot marks." Mother's gaze made the words a question.

Frisby rested her knife and fork. "I saw her. I wish I hadn't. I heard her voice. Like someone

31

calling from across a field. She was so thin. Blood on her mouth. Blood on the front of her dress. A smock. She held out her hand to me. Oh, the horrible boils! With black tops. And she stood awkwardly, Mum, as if..."

"She'd be in pain," frowned Mother, her steak pie steaming, neglected on her plate. Even George had stopped eating.

"I suppose so," said Frisby. "Her hand was towards me, but she was hunched, her elbows away from her body, and stooped, her legs apart, like an old man." Tears surprised Frisby. She rose and drew two tissues from a box.

"What did she say?" said George. "Your spook."

Frisby blew her nose, and sniffed heartily. She tried on a smile for Mother, and sat at the butcher's table. She ate a lot of pie and potatoes. She knew Mother's glance was silencing George. George would grow up one day, Mother assured her.

"If she said anything," sighed Frisby, "I drowned it out with screaming. But she looked so ghastly. And I was still shaking after this morning in the woods. I think it was the same little girl."

"What?"

"Running near the church. Through the trees." Frisby remembered the terrified patter of feet. "Now I think of it – it's funny. Odd."

"Blooming odd!" mumbled George.

"As if she was running on a path I couldn't see – or as if the trees didn't exist."

"Maybe they didn't!" boomed George.

32

"Well," said Mother. "Maybe they didn't when the little girl was alive. I don't suppose there would be trees close around the church when it was in use."

Frisby narrowed her eyes at Mother. "So you believe me?"

"Mmm," said Mother, "but I'm still not pleased about your coat."

"How long have the trees been there?" asked George. "Dad could tell us. He's lived here all his life."

"I don't think your father is that old," said Mother.

"I do know that, Angelique. But he still might —"

"Of course. You're quite right, George. Your father will know. Even if he didn't actually plant them himself."

George grinned, and Frisby giggled. George was really quite handsome in a goofy sort of way.

"Don't strain your brain, Georgie Porgie."

George's hand leapt at Frisby and tugged her curls.

"Enough!" warned Mother.

"I saw ice cream in the fridge," said George.

"No, you didn't. It's for tomorrow."

"You spoil Dad."

"He's worth spoiling."

"I'm glad you're my mother," said George. "I'm off out. See you later, Frizzy."

A rush of air, the door slammed and Mother turned her gaze from the door to Frisby. "Well!" she gasped. "Who would believe it?"

Then she cleared the table, singing on her breath.

A chair wore Frisby's coat. She crushed dried mud from around a button.

Mud crumbs broke on the tiles.

"I hope you know who's going to sweep the floor," sang Mother.

Frisby's brown little fingers crush-crushed, scattering more crumbs.

"Angel!" George in the yard.

"I thought he was gone," said Mother.

The door opened.

"I think you'd better come," said George.

Chapter 7

Tuesday evening. Longman's Reach.

"Come on," said George, as Mother looked at Frisby.

"I'm all right," said Frisby, but her food hung in her stomach.

"Come on!"

"I'm putting on my shoes!" cried Mother, and Frisby realized that Mother was scared too.

"Hurry up, Angel! Come on, Frizzy! You don't mind getting your slippers wet!"

"Yes I do!"

They stepped across the yard, Frisby in her red wellingtons, following George's beckoning arm, walking quietly in the rain when his palm demanded silence.

George stopped, and they peered round him.

"We've left the greenhouse door open," whispered Mother.

"No," said George. "That's what I thought. Blamed you, Angel. Know how fussy Dad is, so I closed it and went into the stable for my bike. When I came out the door was open again."

"You didn't shut it properly!" whispered Frisby. She glanced at George's bicycle against the house wall.

"I thought that too," breathed George, then he said nothing, and Frisby gripped her mother's arm.

"Why," asked Mother, "are we out whispering in the rain?"

George walked towards the greenhouse. Frisby felt very alone with Mother in the emptiness of the yard. And the old red walls stood shoulder to shoulder, peering down on them.

George reached into the greenhouse. He pulled the door shut. He walked hurriedly backwards.

"I heard it click," said Mother.

Rain wet Frisby's cheek, and she let her glance rise to the hillside's bowing grass beyond the willows on the riverbank. When she looked back, the greenhouse door stood open.

"There!" breathed George.

"Oh, it's the wind!" cried Mother, and they stared, Mother and Frisby, as George pulled the door again, *click!* and they waited, blinking; and rain ran cold on Frisby's brow, as the handle moved by itself and the door opened, then the handle turned back as if released from someone's grasp.

"See?" demanded George.

"I didn't know George was so brave!" whispered Frisby.

"I didn't know I wasn't!" gasped Mother. "I always thought, if I ever met a ghost, I'd talk to it! I think I need to sit down!"

"Lean on George!" ordered Frisby.

"It's only a door, Angel!" said George, but his arm secured Mother's shoulders. "Hey!"

Frisby, her heart surging, ran and shut the door again. She stayed, clutching the corner of the greenhouse. Raindrops rolled over her fingers.

"Frisby! Come away!"

Frisby shook her head. "It's awfully cold here!"

The handle turned. "Who are you?" said Frisby to the air.

The door opened. She shuddered. Heat was being sucked from her body. "Oh, Mum! Oh, the despair! Oh death! Death and murder! Mum!"

"Get her!" shrieked Mother, but George was already catching Frisby's arm and dragging her away.

"Inside!" yelled George. "Spooks aren't funny!" And his grasp tightened on Frisby as he forced her and Mother into the kitchen. To Frisby's surprise, he left them.

She stood gasping on the doorstep wiping her rainy face, Mother shivering beside her. They watched George, goofy George, stride back to the greenhouse, one hand in his pocket. He shut the door. His hand came from his pocket. "Sorry, ghost! But Dad's fussy about his tomatoes!"

"He's tying the door shut!" gasped Frisby.

"And I'm fussy about who frightens my sister! Get it!?" His whole body jerked the string tight.

"Half-sister," said Frisby's lips, and a glow of admiration tingled her face.

"Oh, well done!" breathed Mother.

"Howzat!" cried George.

"Pretty good, Georgie Porgie!" whispered Frisby. "It won't stop a ghost!" she yelled.

George came grinning, blond as a Saxon.

Mother stood on tip-toe to see over his shoulder. "Is it still shut?"

George turned. "Still shut," he said. "Well. I'm

off, Angel."

"Your hair's soaking," said Mother.

"My head won't shrink!" shouted George as he dived for his bicycle. He dried the saddle – sort of – with his sleeve.

"Where are you going?"

"Darren's excavating Longman's Reach. Got to do it today he says, in case the weather worsens. You know what the sea can be like. Hah! That was a secret!" He swung astride the bicycle. "Cheerio!"

"Wait," said Frisby.

And because she didn't yell, because her voice rang firm in the rain, George waited, one foot on the muddy yard. "I'm coming," she said.

She turned away as George's mouth opened. She went back, buttoning herself into Mother's coat.

"Can you manage the pedals in your wellingtons?" said Mother. "Are you sure you want to go? You've had a traumatic day…"

Frisby ran to the stable and wheeled out her bike. She checked the tyres. "See you later!"

"Not too late!" called Mother. "It's after six, now!"

Frisby waved, and followed the whirr of George's chain; cutting snakes in the mud around the house; tan trouser knees popping up under Mother's coat, catching raindrops.

"Here," said Darren.

They walked among the dunes and dropped their bicycles.

The rain had stopped, but wind pushed clouds about the sky, and dried the top of the sand.

Frisby walked from the dunes and stared at the sea lying flat and grey, breathing, it seemed, against the beach. The orange sand glowed in the dull light, beautiful as fungus.

"Right here!" came Darren's voice.

"It all looks the same!" exclaimed Frisby running back.

"Further along is much more eroded. The farmers lose a bit more of their fields every year. There's rock in the land here, keeping the sea from eating it away. It hasn't changed much in centuries. We'll square off the sand. One metre squares."

He lifted a plastic carrier bag from his bicycle basket. He didn't seem to mind having a basket at the front. Frisby knew the story that Darren's father had offered him a sports bike with drop handlebars, but Darren refused because he couldn't carry anything on it, and settled happily for this second-hand lady's model advertised in the garage.

He handed wooden pegs to George, and a ball of string to Frisby. "Shove a peg in just there," he said. He measured a metre across the sand with a tape and another peg slid into the sand, then a third in a straight line. Darren paced about carefully, urging the others to stand still, then more pegs went in, forming squares, and Frisby joined them up with string.

"What's the idea?" asked Frisby.

"So we know where we've searched, of course.

And so we can take measurements and photographs."

"If we find anything," said George. "Fat chance!"

"Where's your camera?" asked Frisby.

Darren concentrated on pushing a peg deeper. "Didn't bring it."

"Ha!" from George.

"The weather's too dull. I don't have a flash."

"He means he forgot!"

"Did you bring something to dig with? I want to help."

Darren's glance leapt at her over a smile. "In the carrier."

Frisby found a trowel and a hand-sized gardening fork.

"I thought there'd just be two of us," said Darren. "Start here. Mind the string. We're searching, remember, rather than digging. Imagine there are eggs in the sand. If you uncover something try not to move it until I've noted its position."

Darren tugged a notebook and pencil from his anorak. "I'm glad the rain's off." He knelt on the slope of a dune, and curled over the notebook, pencil sliding carefully.

"Dig in!"

"I'll start in this square." Frisby looked at Darren for approval, but his gaze rose vacantly then returned to the page. Frisby eased the fork into the dry top sand, then deeper into damp sand. She lifted, and the damp sand collapsed between the prongs.

"Try to reach the same depth every time," murmured Darren. "So the bottom of the excavation is level."

"What does it matter!" said George. "You should see Darren's room! His mother has to excavate to find the carpet!"

"It's so I can measure depth."

"Shut up, George," said Frisby. Normally, George's braying was just annoying but now, surrounded by dunes, grass rattling in the breeze and the sea murmuring secrets...

Frisby felt the ancientness of this place. And the idea of digging for the bones of a man dead for six and a half centuries...!

The grass rattled louder and sand blew onto Frisby from the tops of the dunes. She heard the sea groaning against the beach.

"Come on!" muttered George. He dropped the trowel and rubbed grit from his pale hair.

The grass rattled again.

Frisby watched George reach for the trowel.

He hesitated and looked around.

Frisby turned towards Darren.

Darren was staring at the tops of the dunes.

Chapter 8

Longman's Reach. People running.

Grit clattered down on Mother's coat.

"Spooks again?" whispered George.

"Strange," said Darren quietly, "about your greenhouse door. I must take another look." He still stared at the dune tops. He uncurled from the notebook and stood straight.

"What's wrong?" Frisby dropped the fork, stepped over the string and peered around the towering sand. "I can only see a little way."

She darted – like running in tunnels, with the sky for a roof – towards the water, among lower dunes, up a slipping side, gripping grass, standing boldly, Mother's coat pressed tight by the wind, flapping.

She stared along miles of orange sand. Waves frothed, and a green line of seaweed wandered into the distance. Far across the fields the windmill signalled with white arms.

Frisby turned and saw the same view vanishing south, with their bicycle tracks; and in the distance, the roof of the toll house pub showing where the river cut the beach, and where the road ended at the pub, after bridging the river. Seabirds hung in the wind.

Someone was running towards her above the line of seaweed. Frisby's eyes watered.

She wished the grass wouldn't rustle over her

wellingtons. "See anything?" called George.

The tiny running shape divided in two. A man, decided Frisby, and a woman following. "She's fallen!"

Frisby glanced down as George's head rose over the edge of the dune. Darren called, "Is someone there?"

"Oh," said Frisby. "They're gone. The woman fell, but I don't see them now. Anyway, it's nothing to do with us. Let's get down out of the wind."

But George was up, holding onto her, and Darren crowded beside them. Frisby, somehow, didn't mind Darren so close.

"Pretty creepy place!" said George, and Frisby nodded. She shuffled to face the windmill again, and goose bumps froze on her back. She crushed her fingers into George's side making him yell. George wrestled with Darren.

Running away towards the north was a tiny shape that divided in two – a man, with a woman following.

"She's down again!" gasped Frisby, and she stared hard to keep them in sight, but George staggered against her, and when she looked again, nothing moved, but waves and a rising sprinkle of gulls.

"Oh, George! Stop being such a baby! You've missed them again!"

"Spooks! Spooks!"

"What d'you mean?" panted Darren.

"They were there!"

"They were in the other direction a minute

43

ago!" cried George.

"They were there! As if they had run past us! And if you hadn't been behaving like a loony you would have seen them too!"

"Seen who-oo-ooo?"

"Oh, shut up!"

Darren peered both ways, under his hands. "There's nobody."

"There was!"

"Something," agreed Darren, "attracted our attention. We all stopped working at the same moment. What made you stop?" he asked George.

"I don't know. Just a feeling. What does it matter?"

"Our intuition is important. I find it's never wrong. What did you feel, Frisby?"

"I'm not sure. Perhaps ... as if someone was near."

"I thought —" Darren stared carefully along the beach. Frisby saw the windmill waving steadily. " – we were being watched."

"Huh!" said George. "Watched, smotched! There's no one —"

"George, how can you be so stupid! You know what happened with the greenhouse door! You know what I saw! And you talk like an idiot —"

"But I'm a happy idiot!"

"I propose," said Darren firmly, "searching for footprints."

"There won't be any," snapped Frisby. She punched George severely on the arm, and he grinned.

"We should make sure."

"Let's get on with the dig," said Frisby. "I tell you there won't be any footprints. We can look on the way home."

"Yes," said Darren. "We can check to the south on the way home. You carry on here. I'll go north just now. Remember not to move anything you find." And he clambered down, hands sliding on the grass.

"Give us a shout," said George, "if you see any spooks." Darren's head nodded below them, then he hurried among the dunes to the shore. He turned and looked towards the toll house, then waved briefly and walked north.

"I think it'll rain soon," said George. "Let's dig. Keep the professor happy." He slithered down the dune's sandy slope. Frisby watched Darren stride between the seaweed and the water. He seemed to be looking at the sand. "For footprints," she said. "He won't find any."

She returned to the squares. George stabbed the trowel deep, threw sand aside; stab, throw, stab, throw.

"You're supposed to search," said Frisby.

"I'm getting the rhythm."

"But you're supposed to search the sand you're throwing aside."

"It's just sand."

"You don't know!"

"I have X-ray vision. Bzzz-bzzz! Hello." George stopped.

"I've struck gold, Frizzy."

Frisby crouched beside him and forked

carefully. "I feel it. Fingers! Don't move it!"

So twenty fingers busied, wet grains rough on Frisby's skin.

"It's a stone!" groaned George.

A bulge arose in the hole they had dug.

A raindrop splashed onto the bulge leaving a dark brush-stroke.

"I told you it would rain!" shouted George. "Blooming stone!"

Frisby lifted out more sand. The object curved down. More brush-strokes.

She felt the side. "There's a hole."

She withdrew her fingers. "You do it. Carefully."

George burrowed silently.

Rain pattered, hollow on Mother's coat.

"It's too light," muttered George. The object was almost clear. He worked his fingers underneath.

"Careful!"

He eased it loose.

Frisby stood up hurriedly.

George said, "Oh!" and jerked away his hands.

The object which George had said was a stone, stared at the sky, smiling.

Chapter 9

Darren running.

"Oh, cripes!" muttered George.

"So the scrap *was* part of a helmet!" gasped Frisby.

"Meet the owner!" whispered George. "Alas, poor Yorick! He didn't know his dentist well! What a gummy grin!"

"Shut up, George! I'm going to see if Darren's coming! You'd better not move that!"

"Trot along, Frizzy," murmured George, and she left him finger-searching around the skull, raindrops shining on his hair.

She stood on the dune. Waves broke in white lines. Darren's footprints dwindled into the orange and iron evening.

She stared hard where she had seen the figures. Inland, she was conscious of the windmill beckoning. A heron flapped, trailing pink legs. It landed clumsily, then settled on a boulder, death-in-feathers, hunched above the water.

"I don't see him!" she called. Of course, Darren would be among the dunes.

Frisby opened her mouth to shout, then relaxed, for even George hadn't heard her call, and he knelt in a square of string only twenty paces away. Darren, she guessed was half a mile along the beach.

Mother's raincoat touched her hands coldly.

The wind drew a tear across her cheek. Brown curls bounced about her eyes.

"Coo-ee," she whispered. "We've found his head."

The heron lunged; its bill pointed at the clouds, its throat thickened with the corpse of a fish, then it became a statue of itself. "Coo-ee," sighed Frisby. "He's got no brains. He's a six-hundred year-old George." Then she saw Darren and waved both arms.

He walked, ran a little looking back, walked. She waved, dancing. His tiny arm rose. He looked back again then trotted, wandering close to the water then up the shore above the tidal ridge of seaweed. He skipped sideways, as if anxious about what was behind him, then he crossed below the seaweed and ran swiftly.

"I get it," said Frisby. "He was searching for the firmest sand. So he could run easily. Fast."

She watched the dunes beyond Darren, tops green; tunnels where ghosts sleep. "There isn't anything. It's the rain he doesn't like. Maybe he heard me call." Then she remembered she hadn't called.

"I wish it wasn't so cold." She bounced on the spot. She waved again.

From behind a dune, close to Darren, a hand waved.

Then the hand fluttered and drifted low across the sand and settled on the waves. It bobbed up, and slid down on the rolling water.

"Oh!" said Frisby. "My heart! I think I'll shut my eyes for a week. Come on, Darren!" she screamed, and her voice must have reached him despite the wind, for his face popped up, pale beneath his hair.

"'Ello! 'Ello!" grated a policeman's voice, and George's grin appeared beside Frisby's wellingtons. She yelped and stamped her rubber foot on his hand.

"Naughty!" said George. "Is our professor coming?" She pointed. "I've never seen old Darren move like that." George stood beside Frisby, tense. "I'd better go and meet him." He slithered down the dune, and ran steadily.

In the top sand, not yet soaked by rain, George's feet dug craters; below the line of seaweed where the sand stretched damp and firm, his footprints glistened. He met Darren. Frisby heard George's voice. Darren's head shook and he kept running, gasping terribly, pushing George on, George hopping, looking back, arms protesting. Then Darren glanced behind, and he knelt suddenly until George pulled him up, and they approached the dune where Frisby gazed into the distance.

"What's wrong?" she yelled. She ran down the dune.

Darren's brow shone white and moist. He couldn't speak for panting. "There's nothing behind you," she protested.

Darren nodded, urging her to move. "Come on, Frizzy," said George. "Darren's not running for fun." And they helped him among dunes and the familiarity of string squares.

"If there is danger," said Frisby, "we're not any

49

safer here!" She rushed away and climbed the dune. Rain thickened the atmosphere. The sprinkle of gulls rode the swelling waves. The heron seemed to have forgotten it was alive, and the windmill stood drowned in white air, while around Frisby, the grass rustled in the wind.

"There's nothing!" she snapped. She dashed back and found Darren and George crouched at the skull. "There's nothing! Were you trying to frighten me!"

Darren stood up, close to her, still gasping as he spoke. "Sorry! Touch of the horrors along there." He stepped away. "A bit lonely. Like everyone else had gone to the moon. Then that feeling of being watched. You know. One second, empty world; next, eyes feeling you. Like cold maggots on your back. I ran. I ran!" He wiped rain from his cheekbones. "It's not cowardly to run!"

"I never thought —!"

His eyes sprang glances at the tops of the dunes. "D'you think it's too wet to work?"

"Your head won't shrink!" roared George.

"I suppose," gasped Darren, "I *felt* cowardly."

"I wouldn't have walked along the beach for anything!" said Frisby. "Don't worry! Nobody thinks you're a coward. I nearly shattered the greenhouse with my screaming. Don't go on about it."

"I think I'll take another look."

Frisby gaped.

"Come on!" cried George in protest.

"But the skull!" urged Frisby. "Aren't you

50

going to take measurements or something?"

Darren hesitated. "Yes. All right." He stared as if he might see through the dunes and along the endless shore.

"Get your notebook out, then," encouraged Frisby.

Darren's eyes focused on her, and Frisby tilted her head.

"Would you mind?" said Darren. "The skull is terrific. Really. But... We'll cover it up —"

George groaned.

" – and go along the beach. Before it's too dark. All right?"

"Cor!" moaned George.

"Some coward!" sighed Frisby.

Chapter 10

Shining like gold.

"We'll leave the squares," said Darren. He wheeled his bike among the dunes.

"Come on," said George, and Frisby heaved her cycle from the sand, and rubbed sand from the handlebars, wishing she had something to dry the saddle. She would keep Mother's coat under her.

On the beach, rain dashed onto the side of Frisby's head. She cycled – wellingtons knocking her shins – below the line of seaweed. Her tyres printed Dunlop-patterned snakes; wound around the feathered burst of a dead seabird.

They stopped to carry their bikes above the tide-line, avoiding ship-wrecked jellyfish, pink and helpless, until the moon should lift the sea again.

Then they cycled to where Darren's footprints veered up the beach, and they stood, little Frisby, George and Darren, full of life, beneath the hanging sky.

"Is this the place?" said George; but no one answered because no answer was needed.

"You go first," said Frisby, and George rested his bike.

"I'll go," said Darren. "I'm the one who ran away."

"We weren't here to run away." George

grinned at Frisby. "Come on." So they left the bicycles and prowled between the dunes, silent, then chatting when nothing more chilling than wind and rain came to cool their flesh.

"This is a jolly spot right enough!" said George. "No wonder people don't visit. You'd need a rope and a grappling iron to get to the top of these dunes. Hey, Professor, why do they slope towards the land but go up like cliffs facing the water?"

Darren turned from examining a ridge of grass at his feet. "Oh." He looked at Frisby then glanced away. Frisby realized he was shy.

"It's wind from the sea," said Darren, "blowing sand against a tuft of marram – that's what the grass is called. It's like sand-blasting a building to clean it. Cuts around the roots at the seaward side; piles up sand at the land side."

Frisby tipped her head curiously. "You mean these great dunes started as tichy clumps of grass?"

"That's right. And they walk —"

"Walk!"

"Think about it. They wear away at the front, and build up at the back. They walk away from the sea a little bit each year. Lower dunes with no marram on top to protect them, can move yards in a few hours if the weather's stormy. Look at this."

Frisby and George stood gazing down on the green ridge.

"See?" said Darren. "This lump has fallen from the land. This is where the beach comes up to meet the ground. This little cliff is earth, with the oat field on top. Blown sand has eroded it, and grass has fallen, making the ridge. If you come back when you're an old lady —"

"Not me!" snorted George.

" – this will be a dune, and the beach will have eaten away part of the oat field."

"Huh!" smiled Frisby. "The things you know. The earth's pretty sandy." She prodded the broken embankment with her fingers. On top of the embankment, crops nodded behind a wire fence. "Shells here."

"All sorts of things. The history of the countryside is exposed in these layers of earth, if only I could read them. One day, I will."

"The colours are beautiful in the rain," said Frisby. "Too bad we can't keep the stones wet. Look at that! Shining like gold!"

She encouraged George to look, then turned an eye on Darren as he leaned close to the bare wall of history. "You really were scared, weren't you?" she asked.

Darren, crouching, gazed up. Frisby saw nothing in his eyes to make her retreat. She suddenly knew why he was different from other boys: he was too interested in things to waste time showing off.

"It was terrible," he answered at last.

Then he stared at the earth face. His expression tightened. "Get out of the way. Quick!" He crawled, then rubbed with his thumb.

"More chicken bones?" said George. "We could have a pot of soup!"

"George, shut up!" said Frisby.

Darren's breath moved his lips. He sat back, and his eyes glimmered with excitement.

He grinned his bent grin at Frisby. Rain sparkled on his hair.

"Not unless you're a cannibal," he whispered.

Chapter 11

Tuesday evening. Jellyfish.

The oat field rippled.

Wind blew across Frisby's eyes, and she blinked away from Darren, gazing where his thumb had searched.

George whistled a silly tune.

"Don't you see!" Darren rubbed lovingly around the spot of gold. "See!" he hissed.

Frisby and George peered.

"It's a gold ring!" said George.

A dark knuckle protruded. Frisby picked away earth.

"Careful!" Darren's hand clasped hers. He released her instantly.

"It's like the chicken bone," she whispered. She frowned at George. "Someone's wearing the ring!"

"Look," said Darren. "Here. See that line? That's bone. Imagine he's lying down. Then it's just below his fingertips at roughly the same angle —"

"It's his leg!" cried Frisby.

"Further along … his ankle. The foot's gone."

"What d'you mean?"

"The sea took it, I suppose. A spring tide. Or a storm."

"What are we waiting for!" yelled George. "Let's dig him out!"

"No."

"We'll be famous!"

"We'll be shot. No, we must report this. It's too important —"

"We can dig as well as anybody!"

"We would destroy evidence. Every layer of soil – every colour change as the body is uncovered – is evidence. Look at this," said Darren. "Here's where that grass fell away. His head must be in here if his shoulder's towards us... I'll risk a peek."

Darren's fingers dug gently. His mouth moved.

Then his hand came away and he relaxed.

He sat back on his heels. His eyes wrinkled into the tiniest glow of sheer delight.

"Darren?" said Frisby.

"What have you found?" asked George.

"Take a look," said Darren. "Take a really good look."

Above their heads, the oat field rustled, and the wind threw rain between the dunes.

This place, Frisby knew, was where the man and woman had disappeared the second time, as they ran along the beach.

This place was where Darren had experienced the horrors.

She couldn't believe what was buried a hand's depth into the embankment.

Frisby reckoned she'd had enough for one day.

She leaned on George's shoulder, and pushed herself up onto the grassy ground beside the field. She rubbed her palms on the fence's wet wire.

Clouds twisted low in the sky. She saw the windmill and, beyond the oat field, the wood with the haunted church.

The man and woman, she decided to herself, had run along the beach, then through the oat field, then past the church...

"It's time to go home." She jumped down.

"Cover that thing up," said George.

Darren lifted a lump of grass from the fallen ridge, and filled in the gap at the skeleton's head.

They walked away, looking back, fingering dune sides in the closing dusk.

They found their bicycles and rode slowly.

Waves surged, thirsting for their tyres, hissing down the sand. They rode through the jellyfish, and had to stop to wash their wheels; then they cycled past their own dark footmarks where Frisby had looked out for Darren, and where a skull lay in a string square; then towards the bridge; and somewhere in their journey, over the spot where the woman had fallen the first time.

The lights in the toll house pub made the night darker. They sped across the bridge and home. They muttered over bikes in the street, promising Darren – promising each other – to keep this most secret of secrets; a difficult promise, but solemn enough to still even George's braying.

Chapter 12

"What are you up to?" demanded Mother.

Frisby smiled as George innocently poured Mother's coffee. The lounge curtains hung between Frisby and the rushing night. An electric fire warmed the air.

"When George volunteers," remarked Mother, "to make coffee, serves it in a pot, on a tray, with biscuits and," she raised an eyebrow, "clean hands... Well. I know he's up to something. And since you were with him —". Frisby used her eyelashes. " – you are also up to something." Mother smiled firmly. "Aren't you?"

"Oh, Angelique!" scolded George. "We went archaeologizing on the beach! On our bicycles! What could we get up to? Though we did ride through a flock of jellyfish —"

"Oh, George!"

" – by mistake! By mistake, Angel! Hurrying! In the dusk! And the river was high! Wasn't the river high, Frizzy? Like in winter. Foaming through the reeds! If this rain keeps up – down, rather – rain doesn't keep up, does it? If it does it's cloud not rain —"

"George!" groaned Frisby.

"I think he's changing the subject," said Mother, her fingers hovering over the biscuits. She turned her fingers into a fist and relaxed the fist on her lap.

"You're resisting my biscuits!" cried George. "I know! It's because Dad's coming back! Four days in town and you're watching your waistline!"

"Waistlines were made to be watched."

"Oh, very good, Angel!"

Mother lifted a magazine. "I creased the corner of a page," she said. "Here we are…"

"What are you on about?" sighed George.

"Spooks, as you call them. This is an old *Field and Hedgerow*."

"Not one of Dad's treasures!" bellowed George. "Does he know you read them? Does he know you can read?"

"George," said Mother patiently, "if you don't be quiet I'll switch you off at the mains. Thank you." She turned to Frisby. "I remembered where I'd read about your ghost."

Frisby's chest tightened around her heart.

Mother sipped coffee and lifted a biscuit. "Um… Oh, yes. The man writing this says he discovered the story in a newspaper dated 1892, that he found in the drawer of a commode he bought at auction —"

"I didn't think a commode had drawers," said George. "Isn't it for —?"

"It's a chest of drawers," said Mother, "usually with a curved front."

"I thought this story was about ghosts?" said Frisby.

"We're coming to it," said Mother, clenching white teeth through the biscuit, "but people like to know where stories originate. And the newspaper story arose from a hand-written version somebody found in his grandmother's spinet —"

"Is that a sort of potty?" asked George.

"A sort of early piano," sighed Mother, and lifted a biscuit crumb from the magazine. "Oh, look! George! I've eaten a biscuit! Can't you stop! Now I've lost the place. Wait a minute. Yes —"

"Just tell us what it's about, Mum."

"A clergyman. Yes. The Reverend Samuel Bath composed his sermons while walking within sight of Longman's Reach —"

"That's where we were today! Sorry."

"Apparently it was a very hot summer. We're in 1770, by the way. That was the date on the manuscript in the spinet. The path by the hedgerow was dried out to a depth of nearly two feet. Crops were reduced to brown stumps, the hedges to tangled skeletons. The path, being a hundred yards from the beach and normally well drained, now was considerably split and shrunk, so much so that the Reverend Bath couldn't concentrate on his sermon for watching where to place his feet. Then he did concentrate and his walking stick went into a crevice, making him stumble.

"He had difficulty pulling the stick free because the tip stuck – he supposed – on roots. With a mighty haul he released it only to find that the ferrule was missing."

"What's that?" asked George.

"Well, here it means the metal cap on the end, though it can mean the band... Where am I? He searched down with his fingers and broke what he thought was a root, and rescued the ferrule. In his hand was a small twist of extremely heavy wood. He was about to throw it aside, when he looked again, realizing that it was too heavy to be just wood.

"On crushing the object with his fingers, the soil fell away and Samuel Bath was delighted to find in his possession a short length of leather – hard as stone – and a buckle of antique style.

"Much excited – for he was devoted to studies of the past, he reached again into the crevice, but despite damaging his cuff and coat sleeve and the knees of his breeches, he found nothing else.

"So he goes home. Here's the bit. It seemed to the reverend gentleman as he hurried towards the rectory…"

Mother rested the magazine and gazed at the electric heater.

"Mum?"

"This used to be a rectory."

"That's right!" said George. "D'you think he lived here?"

"I'm not sure. It's old enough. Isn't this exciting!" She wiggled into her chair. "Let's see…

"Yes. It seemed … blah, blah, blah … that he heard a child running, but though he looked all around the fields and through the hedgerows, he saw no one. He walked faster, clutching the buckle, taking the shortcut past the church – your haunted church," said Mother to Frisby. "And it seemed that the sea in its murmurings did make sounds not unlike a man in anger, and once –

though anxious to return home – he stopped on hearing what seemed to be a woman's scream; even searching briefly through the copse which protected the church from the sea's winter winds.

"But there's nobody around, so he gets home quickly and cleans the buckle, and is astonished to discover that it's fashioned from gold and decorated with many fine scrolls after the Saxon fashion."

"Golly," said Frisby, and she gazed at George, but George sat silent, his handsome face relaxed, his cup steaming on its saucer.

"A farmer Dowsett," continued Mother, "came asking for a blessing to please his wife, because that good woman had – oh!"

"What's up, Angel?"

"I don't think I read this far last time."

"What does it say?" cried Frisby. "Tell us!"

"It says, ' – because that good woman had sworn an oath that she had truly seen the spirit of a child that cried to her with strange words, and,' *oh, dear!* 'the child's skin was covered over in wicked boils with black crusts —' Frisby, darling! Are you all right?"

"Mu-um! Of course I'm all right!" But her heart jumped uncomfortably, and her cheeks felt slack. "Do get on! I want to know about the little girl!"

"Frisby," said Mother dangerously.

"Sorry. But please...!"

"Hmn," said Mother. "Next. Boils, boils. Samuel leaves the rectory to impart a blessing. By this time the sun is behind the church, turning the trees black, laying shadows and red light across the stunted fields. The air is chillier than he expects and he strides out on his errand. Um... What a lot of words.

"Here we are. They kneel on the bridle path – that is, the Reverend Samuel, and Farmer Dowsett and Mistress Dowsett – at the place where the child appeared, and he prays over them and they sing Psalm Twenty-three which is especially efficacious against ghosts. While he prays, he is conscious of the shadow of the mill sails standing over him – like a great black cross.

"He is uneasy about this, but not concerned, though he admits to supping a pint of ale with the good man before stepping home." Mother gulped her coffee.

George sat back in his chair.

"Now. More blah, blah. He has a lantern. He proceeds past the church and onto the bridge. That must be our bridge – or its ancestor. It's dark now, and rain is cold on his face. He's surprised at the rain, but glad, for the earth needs it.

"He places his hand on the wall of the bridge, and for a moment thinks he has touched something alive, but when he holds the lantern close, he sees only mossy stone. He touches it again and the stone falls into the river. What's this bit about..."

Frisby stared at Mother.

"Is there any more about the little girl?"

"Not yet... I'll start here. He's trying to sleep. His room's upstairs – that might be your room,

Frisby. Goodness! He's trying to sleep, but the rain dashes against the windows persistently, and so like fingernails tapping, that he rises, lights a candle, and opens the curtains. But he sees only the reflection of the candle and a white movement which is certainly his own face.

"So he went to bed."

Mother let the pages fall shut.

"Is that it?" said George.

"There must be more!" cried Frisby.

"Continued next week," beamed Mother.

"Potties!" muttered George.

Chapter 13

The Black Death.

"Not to worry," said Mother. "George is sure to have the next copy in his den."

"I'll look!" cried George.

"Be careful with your cup!"

"It's empty, Angel!"

"Be careful of your father's things!"

Bang! said the door. "Yes, oh, Mother!" came muffled from the hall.

"He's started calling you 'Mother'," commented Frisby.

"I hope not," said Mother grimly. "I don't want people thinking I'm that old!" She smiled. "What's Darren's latest secret?" She wriggled to the edge of her chair. "He hasn't got a girlfriend?"

"Oh, Mum," grinned Frisby. "It's a real secret," she said quietly, glancing at the oak door.

The handle gleamed brassy bright.

George would be finding the key to his father's glass-fronted bookcase. It would be minutes before —

The door crashed open. "What date's that magazine, Angel? Right! Won't be long!" The door slammed, pushing cool air across the room.

"Cripes!" said Frisby, and they laughed.

"Well?" said Mother.

"It *is* a secret. And I promised Darren."

"Oh." Mother lifted a biscuit, opened her mouth, blinked and put the biscuit back.

"Is the greenhouse door still shut?" asked Frisby.

"Yes. Oh, yes! I think so. I only looked once. From the window. Plenty of housework you know! Getting the place in shape for George."

"You didn't dust the den!"

"Just a bit. That's how I remembered where I'd read about your spooks – ghosts. Isn't it strange? I suppose she had bubonic plague."

"Ugh. That sounds horrible! Who had bubonic plague? What is bubonic plague?"

"The Black Death. The little girl. Buboes are swellings under the arms and between the legs. People came out in lumps all over. And the lumps had black tops – the Black Death."

"But that's terrible!"

"It wiped out millions of people all over Europe."

"And you think the little girl ... I've never seen anything so awful. The worst thing, Mum ... the worst thing was her hand, red and swollen and with these black crusts... She held it towards me, wanting help. Now she's been dead hundreds of years."

Frisby poured half a cup of coffee. It was cool now, but gulping it prevented tears. "Thirteen forty-nine!" she gasped.

"Thirteen forty-eight," said Mother, "the Black Death struck England."

"Darren thought thirteen forty-nine... Oh."

"Another secret?"

Frisby nodded, sighing. "Oh, creep, creep," she said. "Secrets about everything. I suppose he's not so bad. He's shy."

"Yes," said Mother. "I know children who are loners because they are too bright or because their cleverness lies in a non-academic direction. They're simply not interested in the school's curriculum. They want to know about, well, archaeology, for example."

"Maybe I'm clever like that," sighed Frisby.

"Well, whatever it is, I hope it earns you money. I know what it's like being without, and when —"

"Oh, Mum! Not a lecture on job prospects! I've told you – if I don't get a job I'll sell my drawings! I am working at them! I'm doing a summer project on 1920s' fashion... I could do a drawing of the little girl! She must be lonely. Wandering from the shore to the church, then from the church to here – I wonder if she runs from here back to Longman's Reach. A circle of running, on and on... Looking for help, and no one paying the least attention. How awful. Oh, Mum! she could be in the yard now!"

"Sit down," said Mother. "If she's been there all that time another night won't matter."

"You're heartless!"

"Were you going to invite her in?"

"Oh, no!" Frisby smiled. "I don't know. Just tell her we care. We could do that! Let's! Oh, Mum! Come on!"

"Now?"

"Of course now!"

"It's very late."

"We'll take Georgie Porgie. If he's not guzzling your George's Glenmorangie."

"George doesn't drink," said Mother firmly. "All right! I'm coming!"

Frisby ran through the kitchen and opened the back door.

Rain sparkled in the light from the doorway.

A car horn peeped and headlights blazed from beside the house into the yard.

"Here's your George!" yelled Frisby. "Warn George in the study, Mum!" And she ran in her slippers through the brilliant rain and swung wide the door of the Small Barn.

The car rolled inside, pressing light around the walls. The lights vanished, and a man's voice rose above the drumming raindrops. "Hello, Frisby! What's happened to the weather? Your mum here? Anything wrong? You're up awfully late."

"Hello," said Frisby. She really did like Mother's George, but her shyness – even after more than two years – meeting his shyness, kept them apart.

"George!" Mother came running into the barn. "You're early." He welcomed her with his arms, and Frisby stared at the fall of light from the kitchen door full of silver spears.

Then the car boot opened and shut, the door of the Small Barn groaned, and they dashed, all three, through the mud.

"George in bed?"

"Why are you early?" cried Mother.

"Wrapped things up quicker than we thought."

George led them into the lounge, where he dumped his suitcase and threw a newspaper into a chair. "And I decided I'd rather be here than stuck in London."

Frisby turned to the newspaper as kissing began.

"That's enough," said Mother, a smile in her voice.

The newspaper was dated the following day.

Frisby unrolled it.

The headline was political and didn't interest her. A smaller heading attracted her eye.

"Coat off," said Mother. "Tea?"

"Yes, Angel. Thanks."

"Frisby, you've left muddy footprints on the carpet."

"Mum."

"I'm going to make tea for George. Are you finished with the coffee?"

"Mum!" Frisby thrust the paper at her mother.

"What is it? You look as if you've seen..." Mother blinked.

"What's up?" George leaned towards the paper. "Oh, you mean – it's not as bad as it sounds. Nobody's dropped the Bomb —"

"Oh, George!" cried Mother. "You don't understand! You don't know what's happened here today! And now this!" She stared at the paper.

She sat suddenly, on the arm of a chair.

Then she read out the heading.

"'Black Death Strikes Norfolk'," she whispered.

Chapter 14

Tuesday bedtime.

"Hello, Dad! What are you doing home? What's wrong? Frizzy's gone almost pale. We borrowed this magazine from your collection. Hope you don't mind —"

"What *is* going on? Hello, George. Which magazine is it? Oh. Be sure to return it to its correct place. I'm taking my suitcase upstairs – nobody we know," he gasped, "has caught the plague?"

"Oh, no!" cried Mother.

"Plague?" barked George.

"Perhaps there will be some tea, Angelique, when I come down." George's father hesitated, suitcase in hand. "Nobody's ill?"

"No! Oh, my!"

"I'll be down in five minutes then."

"What's up?" asked George, as his father clumped out. He gazed at the newspaper over Mother's shoulder.

"I'll make the tea," said Mother, and left George with the paper against his chest.

"I don't get it," said George.

Frisby pointed at the heading. "Read it out!" she said.

"Plague? Hold on. It's very short. 'Two people in Nanton' – cripes! – 'have bubonic plague! The plague has appeared many times in England's

71

history, but the most destructive epidemic was in the fourteenth century when 25,000,000 people are believed to have died throughout Europe. It is known as the Black Death...'" George lowered the paper. "I don't get it, Frizzy. What's this got to do with anything? Darren's old man must be involved. Right here in Nanton, eh? Today. We'll all have to be sprayed. And injected. And our heads shaved —"

"Oh, George! Two people have actually caught this! Does it say anything else?"

George scanned the paper. "Seems there's hardly any plague left in the world... 'Even though it's extremely contagious and infectious this isolated outbreak will be easily contained, and with antibiotics easily treated...' There you are! An epidemic of two! But so what?"

"George, Mum's just said that the little girl had bubonic plague." She explained Mother's thoughts.

"Wow!" said George. "What a crazy day! The chaps at school will think I'm as dotty as Darren. I'd like to know what caused the spook to appear – and did the spook cause this bit of Black Death. Or did the Black Death cause the spook? Or was the spook —"

"Stop calling her a spook, George!"

"You know who I mean. Was she maybe trying to warn us —"

"Warn us!" whispered Frisby.

"Let's see what Dad's magazine says."

"Don't tear it!" hissed Frisby as George dug at the pages.

"Here! 'Haunted Norfolk. The Strange Tale of the Reverend Samuel Bath, Continued from —'"

"Get on!"

"It's by Willoughby Chough. What a name! Imagine being called Willoughby Chough at school —"

"George!"

"Chuff-chuff! Or Willow-bough! Hang on! Isn't he something to do with the museum? I think Darren knows him. I'm sure he does."

Mother came in with a tray, a silver teapot steaming on it and a round of sandwiches. George's father had his arm across her shoulders.

"Finding what you want in my magazine?" he asked anxiously.

"We won't damage it, Dad!"

"I've sliced the end off the ham for your sandwich," said Mother.

"Best bit! Did I hear Willie Chough's name?"

"Ice cream for tomorrow!" cried George. "In your honour!"

"Angel knows how to look after me," said his father smugly, and Frisby looked away as his film-star face warmed on Mother.

Frisby wasn't jealous. She was embarrassed at Mother and George's father being so close. But she was glad. Her own father had shown little affection.

"It's like having teenagers for parents," she said to herself, and felt her face glow, as one teenager raised his eyebrows at her, and the other gazed, eyes round and shining.

"Sorry," said Frisby. "Just thinking."

73

"Frisby. If you can find someone to love as much as I love your mother…"

"I don't mind," whispered Frisby. "Really."

"Are you trying to tell us!" cried George at his father, "That you know Willoughby Chough?"

"Since school. And if you'd ever been in the museum you would know him. You can't avoid him, though people try. He was a nasty boy. Talked about fairies —"

"Sorry?"

"Fairies, George. And ghosts. Anything on the lunatic fringe —"

"Spooks aren't lunatic!" cried George.

"You've changed your tune," laughed his father.

"We have evidence," said George. "Piles of it."

"Shouldn't you two be in bed?" Manly fingers tightened on Mother's hand.

"Don't you want to hear our evidence! Frizzy was so scared that Darren's dad sent her for a snooze!"

"What?"

Frisby looked away from his kindly gaze.

"I think I'd better hear this. You talk. I'll eat."

So with George braying, and Mother refereeing, Frisby told the story – trying very hard to say nothing about the helmet or the skeleton, for these were Darren's secrets. And as she talked, events came together in her mind.

She realized that the dead ran – as Mother had said – from Longman's Reach to the church, because they had run that way as living people; though why they had run, nobody knew.

And Samuel Bath's buckle had not come from the grave of the man in the helmet, or from the skeleton, for they were both on the beach, and the buckle had clung to the clergyman's walking stick a hundred yards inland.

Then George exploded with the idea that Samuel Bath had caused the haunting in his time, by taking the buckle, for hadn't he heard the child running, the man raging and the woman screaming? And hadn't the farmer's wife seen the little girl? Which meant that the buckle was part of the mystery...

Frisby tried to remember something Darren had said...

Then Mother suggested it was natural that the little girl came to their house for help, because it once was the rectory; but George's father doubted this, because the house was not fourteenth century; then he was silent.

Frisby sat, lips open, prepared to tell about the skeleton, then she remembered Darren's face as they huddled over bicycles in the road, and shut her lips on the secret that was a real secret.

Mother stared at her husband. She touched his hand. He looked at the sandwich between his fingers. He ate, then rose slowly and wandered into the kitchen.

Frisby followed.

He stood in the open doorway, rain shimmering, wetting the floor tiles.

He made room, and Frisby stood beside him. His hand sat light on her shoulder.

"Some story," he said.

"I was going to tell her we were sorry," said Frisby. "That's why I was outside when you drove up."

"You were really scared?"

"Huh! When I first saw her! But not now. Not really. She was so helpless!"

Rain beat on the mud, like wet diamonds.

"I'm sorry!" whispered Frisby into the darkness that huddled beyond the kitchen's glare. "I'm sorry I couldn't help. What do you want?" she called. "Tell us what you want!"

The fingers on her shoulder tightened. Frisby gazed up at the man who was her mother's husband.

She saw through the handsome face, and found kindness.

She thought of her father, with his intelligence and scowling logic.

She knew why Mother was in love.

"I'd like to look at the greenhouse door, but it's rather wet. Some August." He munched the last of his sandwich. "Tomorrow. Tomorrow will do, eh?"

Frisby touched his cheek. He blinked down at her. Her caress stuck on his bristles. She knew he hadn't shaved since morning. She pulled his face down and kissed the masculine jaw.

"Yes," she said. He was her George now. "Tomorrow."

Chapter 15

Wednesday morning. Murder.

Sunlight stood in the kitchen.

Bacon and sausage tempted Frisby's vegetarian palate, but she bravely made do with Rice Krispies and toast with honey.

"Steam's rising off the yard," commented her new George. He left the back door open and fresh summer air rushed in to investigate people's legs.

"Thank goodness the rain's off!" exclaimed Mother. "The way it was coming down last night, I thought the house would float away. Did you give George a knock, Frisby?"

"Yes, but he's dead."

"Be a dear, and tell him breakfast's ready."

"Oh, Mum!" But Frisby went yelling up the stairs and hammered on George's door.

"Coming!" bellowed George, and he rushed out, tucking in his shirt tail, down the stairs two at a time, crashing into the kitchen, Frisby at his back. "Morning, Angel! Dad!"

"Hello, George. Well, no ghostly fingers undoing your string." He held up the greenhouse string and dropped it into the bin.

"Great morning!" cried George. "Hello! Here's Darren."

"Come in, Darren," said Mother, as Darren hesitated on the doorstep. He wiped his feet and smiled his bent smile. "Could you eat some bacon?"

"Well…"

"Sit in!" yelled George.

"My father left early this morning." Darren's green glance slid over Frisby, touched on Mother. "By the time I got up, Mum had gone too."

"Help yourself to toast," said Frisby and she saw her George's eyebrows rise, then his mouth pulled down with approval.

"You didn't…" Darren's thin palm enclosed a knife. He spread toast.

"Not a word" said George. "Listen, Darren, is your dad involved in the plague? We read about it —"

"Yes —"

"Bacon," said Mother. "You'll manage the egg?"

"Yes. Thank you."

"Angel says Frizzy's ghost had plague —"

"One egg enough?"

"Oh, yes. Thank you." Darren's head bent to the food.

Frisby smiled at his black tufted hair. She remembered George last night talking about Willoughby Chough's possible nicknames, and wondered why Darren wasn't called "Tufty". Then she thought, he's not popular enough.

"I heard him come off the phone," said Darren. "He said to Mum, 'Sounds like another one.' Then he ran. He's worried, I think, because he has no idea where it's coming from."

"Is it really curable?" asked Frisby. "Do you know?"

"Oh, yes. Though it's highly contagious."

"It is safe for you to come here?" asked Mother.

"Frizzy doesn't want her head shaved!"

"Sunlight kills the bacilli," murmured Darren. "I heard Dad yesterday wishing for better weather."

"Plenty this morning," said Frisby's George. "Pass the honey, Frisby. Thanks. Oh." He looked towards the open door. "The sun's gone. I was hoping to start on the greenhouse today."

"Aren't you going to work, Dad?"

"I'm still in London, officially."

Frisby rose and shut the door. "It's too cold now," she said, then remembered the story of Samuel Bath, and went into the lounge. She returned, carrying the magazine carefully.

"Do let me eat," said Mother. "Tell Darren the first part."

"Yes!" said George, and he told Darren. When he mentioned the buckle, Frisby thought that Darren's glance moved too quickly from George's face. But she couldn't think why Darren would feel guilty about a buckle described in an old magazine.

"I'll read the next part," said Frisby.

"Don't dip the pages in the butter," urged her George.

"Sorry. Here it is. It's terribly pompous."

"The style of centuries past," said Mother, "though toned down somewhat by Willoughby Chough. If you'll give me a minute I'll read it."

"He's using words I've never heard."

79

"I'll bet Darren knows them!" said George. "Hey, Darren, what's *cupidity* —?"

"Cut it out, George," said his father.

"Greed," mouthed Darren. A tiny flush of red flooded his cheek bones.

"There you are!"

"Give me the magazine." Mother wiped her fingers on a napkin. She said, "Hmn," like a school teacher. "He goes to bed. Samuel Bath. Three paragraphs about his feelings. He sleeps, eventually, and dreams. He is a child – a girl – in a tiny room with a dead baby lying stiff in a box of straw. Rats try to eat the baby and she thrashes at them with a besom —"

"What's a besom?" asked Frisby.

"A broom. The kind witches fly on."

"Ho. Ho."

" – but the rats run over her feet and she is bitten, though she continues to strike. A man enters and together they clear out the vermin. He takes the baby away. The girl is hiding among the dunes now – um... Oh, I see. The dream has changed. Her flesh burns with pain from decaying buboes —"

"Oh, Angel!" sighed her husband. "I'm eating."

"Sorry. She can smell the corruption of her own body, and bleeds from her mouth and every other part. But she has suffered now for eleven days and knows she might live, but her father... Hold on. Yes. Samuel Bath has the girl's memory. Her father is a mercenary. His spirit brims with greed and violence. He is paid by the lord of the manor to destroy anyone carrying the Great Pestilence. We were right – she did have the plague —"

"What's pestilence?" asked Frisby.

"Short for pest!" snorted George.

"You should know!"

"Pest," smiled Mother, "*actually*, is short for pestilence. But the Great Pestilence was another name for the Black Death.

"The child's father would kill even her, for gold. She is hiding on the beach when she hears her mother screaming at her to run. She runs feebly staying out of sight among the dunes. She rests once, looking back and sees her mother fall.

"The miller's family are her friends, so she leaves the beach and hurries through the fields. The crops lie beaten to the ground by summer rain. The air is cold for the sun has not shone during several weeks. The miller chases her away. Oh, the things people did because of fear!

"She decides to seek sanctuary in the church – your haunted church, Frisby. She approaches, but her father shouts and she knows he has seen her. She flees to the church door, but it is locked...

"Yes, I remember," Mother frowned at no one in particular, "people paid gold to the church for protection against the plague, but the clergy would shun the gold that showered over their walls. I'm sort of quoting something."

She explored the page again.

"The child plays a gruesome game of hide-and-seek among the gravestones. This is awful! She turns to plead for her life. She can go no further. Her mother is screaming somewhere in the fields. Her father closes, sword creaking from its scabbard —"

"Creaking!" whispered Frisby.

" – grotesque in an old helmet of bronze and leather. She raised her hand in pleading, but…"

Darren turned towards George at the mention of the helmet.

"Everyone finished eating?" asked Mother.

Nods.

"He cuts her in half."

"Angelique!" said George.

"His own girl?"

"Oh, Mum!"

Darren's eyes slid, feeling – guessed Frisby – what the girl felt; or the man.

"It was a terrible time," said Mother.

"But your own child!"

"Come on!" said George. "Everyone enjoys a bit of grue. Short for gruesome," he explained. "Is there more?"

"Plenty about his feelings when he wakes up. They did go on, in those days. Samuel Bath is overjoyed at the fine quality of the buckle. The cook gives him a row for neglecting breakfast… This sounds creepy.

"The day being cool and overcast, he decides to work on his sermon indoors. Indeed clouds roll so thick from the sea that he is forced to light a lamp in order to write. The sky is lurid, the only brightness hanging low over the water, and sickly yellow it is. He works for a long time, pausing frequently to examine the buckle and take pleasure in his possession of it.

"The sexton brings wine. Samuel thinks the wine is corked, then realizes —"

"What does it mean – corked?" asked Frisby.

"It means the wine's sour," explained her George, "because the cork has come loose and let the air in."

"Samuel Bath realizes it isn't the wine, but the atmosphere in his study, and he hunts around with the lamp, sniffing, bidding a servant look in the garden in case carrion is outwith the study window.

"But nothing is found. The stench is so bad he must remove himself thence to another part of the house. Wow!" gasped Mother. "I could take some hot tea!"

"I'll get it," said Frisby.

"I'll get it," said her George and reached the kettle first.

"He carries the lamp to his bedroom and sits at the window, desk on his knee —"

"Desk on his knee!"

"Ssh!"

" – and though disturbed in his thoughts, gets on with the sermon with only the hiss of the lamp and the scratching of his pen for company. By luncheon the clouds range purple, in solid rows across the sky, and he eats sitting at his bedroom window – for the smell persisted downstairs – and lightning stood between the clouds and the sea, though no sound of thunder reached him.

"A rat runs from beneath the larch tree..."

Mother tipped her head at Frisby. "That stump you can see from your side window. Is it a larch?"

"You really think my bedroom was Samuel Bath's bedroom!"

"Seems so. He is about to ring for a servant, when the rat runs onto the grass. It falls, and the clergyman stares very hard, for the creature dissolves – oh, thank you, darling." She sipped fresh tea.

"Oh, Mum!" breathed Frisby.

" – dissolved, it says."

"Get on, Angel!"

" – dissolved. He stood up, thinking he saw the rat's skeleton, but he dropped his tray, and when he looked from the window again, the rat had disappeared.

"He hurried downstairs and into the garden. He felt quite ridiculous – a God-fearing clergyman with all the dignity of the Church at his back – crawling under a larch like a hound to the scent. But he found no blade of grass broken or bent by the rat's passage.

"He realizes that the rat was not a real animal, but a warning. Though a warning of what, he could not conceive, but his thoughts did fly to his precious buckle." Mother beamed. "Continued on page thirty-one."

She searched. "Oh."

"What is it?"

She looked at her husband. "I thought you took such care of these." She held up the magazine. A quarter of the page had been cut away.

"Someone," suggested Darren, "has cut out an advert on the back."

Mother looked. "You're right."

"Read what *is* there!" urged George. "Come on!"

"Very well," said Mother. She drank tea. "These things do happen."

"*Angel!*"

"Angel!" mimicked Mother. "All right, all right. Stop interrupting you two." George let his eyes glaze at Frisby. "There's only a bit of a column left. Rum-tiddle-um-tum. What a lot of words. He has the sexton saddle his mare. He is going for a think.

"He follows the path by the river. He looks back at the house. All the windows are open despite the coolness of the weather, to let out the stench. The buckle is very much in his mind. Four paragraphs, this time, about his doubts. He wonders if greed has entered his soul. He stops where he found the buckle. And a hundred paces off, the sea sighs like a lost soul. The mare dances nervously. Samuel Bath turns in the saddle but observes nothing.

"The mare's eye rolls white. He pats her neck, and sings a hymn, partly to calm the mare, partly to strengthen his own spirit. He feels someone is staring into his back.

"That's a terrible feeling, isn't it?" said Mother.

"Angel!"

"Don't blame me, George," beamed Mother. "That's all there is."

Chapter 16

Wednesday morning. An evil little man.

Groans burst around the butcher's table.

"You are a beast, Angel," grumbled George. "You knew it would end there!"

"Oh, well," said his father, "it doesn't really matter —"

"Dad!"

"Disappointing, not hearing the end of the story. But hardly a catastrophe."

"But we saw the man and woman on the beach!" cried Frisby. "At least I did. George was so busy fooling he missed everything —"

"Fool, fool!"

"Georgie Porgie!"

"We'll go to the museum." Darren's voice caused silence. "I noticed the article was written by Willoughby Chough." He nodded at the magazine on Mother's plate. "He'll tell us the end of the story."

His glance flicked from George to Frisby, and for a moment his black pupils held her in discs of emerald fire.

Something sank from Frisby's heart to her stomach; not despair; an excitement, rather; and she blinked away, panting suddenly.

"Come on!" yelled George. "You coming, Frizzy?"

"It's raining," said his father.

"Put something on your head," cried Mother, as they rushed to get ready, Frisby in Mother's coat, George, a dry left-over of toast floating on his hair.

"What are you doing!" laughed Mother.

"Something on my head!" bellowed George, and Frisby followed him outside, Darren saying thank you for his breakfast and Mother assuring him it was all right and to return for lunch if his parents were out, and Darren thanking her for *that* —

"Come on!" yelled George. "You're never as polite to me!"

They wobbled around the house, George heaving down on his pedals, balancing toast.

"Geo-orge!" protested Frisby.

"It's only sensible to have something on your head!"

They sizzled along, rain tapping Mother's hood, Darren's jumper sparkling, Frisby trying not to giggle at startled glances from the pavement; George solemn beneath his toast.

They passed Mason's department store, Frisby craning to see the teenage fashions, then piled the bikes against the museum railing and chained them with a single chain.

"You can't go in with that!" giggled Frisby, and Darren grinned.

"Angel said..." George disappeared into the museum, and Frisby caught the heavy glass door cold on her palm.

Inside, George was professoring, hands a-wiggle at his back, before a granite millstone. The toast, rain-softened, nestled in his hair.

Frisby smiled, and sighed behind a tall glass case. Shelves of pottery waited to be looked at; but she watched Darren curved over a giant lump of coral. His fingers flitted on its pitted surface, as if it might be alive, a grey animal, with hidden limbs waiting to embrace him.

His face, dipped in shadow, relaxed. His palms closed on the coral's flanks and his eyes shut. It seemed his weight went onto his hands.

Frisby moved. Was he ill? Then he straightened, a shudder quivering his shoulders. Frisby knew he had experienced his strange ability to taste the past.

She walked from behind the glass case, intent on sharing the secret —

A door, half-buried down a flight of stairs squealed open, and a man bobbed in – fat, and small in a suit, cheeks squeezed into a smile. The smile touched Frisby like a damp caress, and she stopped walking; but the man came up the steps, feet slapping, as if to state his authority.

He said, "Hah!" and his head jerked at Darren. Lights slid on his scalp; his eyes snapped a glance at George, and Frisby smiled as George joggled wet toast secretly in his palms.

"Together are we? Hello, young man. What are we interested in today? Just browsing? Welcome. You're welcome." But his eyes, thought Frisby, gave her nothing – certainly not welcome. But, she decided, he would *take*...

Darren said, "This is Mr Chough. Frisby and George."

"Yes, yes. Pleased, I'm sure. Pleased to see young people interested in the past." Willoughby Chough's glance landed on George and leapt away.

George's hands hung cupped as if nursing a snowball. Frisby held her breath to capture a giggle, and the little man's eyes glittered from above his bunched cheeks.

But Darren was talking about the story in the *Field and Hedgerow* and Willoughby Chough turned his back on two foolish youngsters and nodded vigorously at Darren. So Frisby prodded George towards the door and they stepped into the rain and the relief of laughter clashed with a roaring bus, and George emptied his hands in the gutter.

"Oh!" gasped Frisby. "Mr Chough doesn't like us!"

George held his hands for the rain to wash. "Chuff-chuff," he sighed.

"Behave, now. Let's go in. And don't dare look at me, or I'll explode!" And she led George inside, trying not to think of wet toast.

But the displays stood deserted.

"Where are they?" said Frisby.

George gazed down the staircase. "That door looks awfully shut," he murmured. So they wandered, adding fingermarks to glass cases, spreading breathy mist between themselves and coin displays, mineral samples...

"I wish he'd hurry up," sighed Frisby. The silence in the museum was brittle, full of self-respect, ready to be indignant at water dripping from her sleeve, or at George's goofy boredom.

The door squealed and Darren's drone was shattered by Willoughby Chough's leather-slapping feet.

"It's not all that important," insisted Darren. "We really don't need help. I didn't mean to mention…"

"He hasn't blabbed!" gasped George.

"But any archaeological find could be worthwhile! More than worthwhile! Any museum would benefit —"

"Really, it's nothing," said Darren. "Sheep bones, I expect!" He advanced on George and Frisby, Willoughby Chough quick-footed at his side, eyes angry over smiling cheeks. "Let's go, you two!"

"But you're not qualified! I mean you're still a schoolboy…"

Darren turned suddenly. Frisby gaped as he stared down on the little man, and Willoughby Chough stepped back almost stumbling onto the coral.

Then Darren marched, thrusting the glass door, and Frisby said, "Thank you," – though what she was thanking the man for she didn't know – and hurried after George.

"You didn't tell him!" groaned George.

Darren thumped the museum wall with his fist.

"I didn't mean to! I mean, I thought he would help. But the look in his eyes! Sheer greed! He could have slit my throat. D'you know he would stick it in his mouldy museum? The place is short of funds. Money and glory…"

He stopped talking.

"What is it?" asked Frisby.

Darren stared between Frisby and George. "I put my hands on the coral," he said, "and the feeling I got... Willoughby Chough must have touched it thousands of times as he walked past. Don't you see? He's left an imprint of himself. I wondered why such horrible sensations came off coral... What an evil little man."

Darren glanced back.

Frisby said, "Oh!" for Willoughby Chough stood beyond the glass door, fat and staring.

"Come on," said George, and he unlocked the bicycles, Darren drying his saddle with a khaki handkerchief, George sweeping away water with his palm, Frisby sitting on Mother's coat, creaking and wheel-spinning into the traffic, escaping from Darren's mistake.

And Frisby wondered if they had the right to keep such a secret. She recalled Darren's fingers digging towards the skeleton's head. Her skin thrilled again at the memory of earth crumbling, exposing a glow of gold, and set in the gold, the deep-coloured shine of precious stones.

Certainly, Willoughby Chough was not the man to tell, but perhaps someone else? After all, she thought, it's not every day you find a dead king.

Chapter 17

Wednesday morning. Longman's Reach.

They rested at traffic lights.

"What about Samuel Bath?" said Frisby above the groan of car brakes. She glanced back at an orange mini.

"Chough wouldn't say."

"But why not?"

"I'd let slip about the bones. He wouldn't listen. Wanted to know where the bones were — Here we go."

The lights turned green and they eased away. The mini roared. Frisby scowled as exhaust wafted from behind her.

"So the museum was worse than a waste of time!"

"'Fraid so!"

"I wouldn't trust that man! Anyone as fat has to be greedy!"

They cycled singly because of overtaking traffic. Frisby noticed the mini had not overtaken, and looked back.

The little car signalled and pulled towards the kerb. She rode carefully beside a van, then looked again, but a bus shut off her view. Surely not? She had Willoughby Chough on the brain.

They sped through quiet streets and silent rain.

Frisby said, "We must be really certain."

She stopped cycling and the others braked,

slightly ahead.

"I'm certain," said Darren. "Anyway, we can't dig him up."

"Just a little dig," sang George. "Just a little-dig-with me-ee!"

"I can't really believe that we've found the king," said Frisby. "Shouldn't we at least see that he's all right."

"I suppose so." Darren smiled at her, then glanced away.

Frisby realized he was embarrassed at being asked to decide. She looked away, back along the road.

A pale red car appeared round the corner and pulled in; or perhaps it was orange, thought Frisby vaguely, but rain was misting down, shading away colour. Darren's jumper hung dark with water.

"Let's go then!" she cried, and they whirred over tarmac.

The air freshened as the arms of the town released them into countryside.

The river sang to willows on the banks. George in his anorak complained of heat; then they rode onto the bridge at the toll house pub, propped the bikes, locked, at the bridge wall, for the sand – as George had just discovered – slid from under turning wheels.

Darren squeezed rain from his sleeves, pressed water from his hair leaving his head as smooth as a pebble – drawing a cackle from George, a grin from Frisby; then they walked above the seaweed, Darren noticing out loud that last night's downpour had battered flat their footprints.

And the sea lapped grey along the distant sand, nodding a bottle onto the beach, pawing the seaweed's fingers. The sky sat invisible, a wet brightness, and rain, fine rain, swallowed the sea, dissolved the land.

And this haunted shore invaded Frisby's soul, so that she wanted to weep for the dead; to cry out to the spirits that lingered among the dunes; to ask forgiveness for being helpless, and bid them rest with the sand among their bones.

She turned and stared back towards the toll house, pretending her tears were rain.

She cried out – ghosts in her memory, "Among the dunes! Something moved!"

But only the dark grass clung on dune tops, and sea birds plodded.

"No spooks, Frizzy!" cried George, but his voice rang soft, as if the sea's flat silence affected even his explosive verve.

So they walked, George picking up a stone, drop-kicking it into the water, Darren alert to the sand passing under their feet. Frisby turned around blinking at their churned trail of footprints.

"Here," said Darren, and George followed him among the dunes.

Frisby stood on the beach.

"I left the tools in my saddlebag" came Darren's voice. "Though we won't dig here just now. We must go and look at the king. Make sure he's all right..."

Darren's voice droned, baffled by the dunes.

Frisby gazed from inside Mother's coat to where the pub hid in the finely beaded air.

The smell of the sea cooled her nostrils and she smiled behind her brown cheeks, then daringly – for her heart surged – she walked back, watching the dunes' sandy faces, their green hair, looking for movement —

She caught it.

She stopped.

A head?

Showing, then hidden.

She hurried to the land side of a dune and clambered up a slope, standing, a small girl standing tall like a woman, seeing through the misting rain to where the bridge held their bikes by a chain.

A smile lay tight over her mouth as her eye found an orange blob.

She ran down the slope, saying, "George! George!"

She found George, crouched with Darren in the string squares.

"Spooks?"

"Willoughby Chough!" snorted Frisby. "The little beast has followed us!"

Chapter 18

A touch of plague.

"Let's bash him!" George jumped up. "Let's roll him in jelly fish! Let's float him over to Holland!"

"Oh, George!" sighed Frisby.

"He'll find this site," said Darren, and they stood, dismayed at their footprints. "Pull the pegs out. Hurry! Mind the string! This way! Follow me! We'll go towards him! Lay out the squares again! He might not come this far!"

Frisby ran after Darren and George. They chose another place among the dunes, stretched the string into squares, pushed in the pegs. She was pleased at Darren giving orders.

"Trample around!" cried Darren softly. "I'll dig."

And he dug with his fingers into the wet sand, then he said, "That's enough you two! Go back to the real site. Scatter sand over the footprints! Then we'll dash around! Confusion to the enemy!"

"Hoofmarks in the dunes!" brayed George, and Frisby followed him. They threw sand to cover the peg holes and footmarks; but the sand fell in lumps, refusing to scatter.

"It's not very good," said George.

"Dry sand!" hissed Frisby, and she dug into the dune-side where grass overhung catching the rain. So they threw dry sand, which spread in the air, blanketing evidence, lying pale, gradually darkening with moisture.

"Good!" said George. "Confusion!" And he wiped gritty palms down Frisby's face, and she yelled, and flew after him.

Rain busied the air. The sea murmured, its voice beside Frisby as she ran in the roofless tunnels. She stopped running, smiling; George came cautiously, grinning, and she smiled until he came close then kicked his ankle.

George said, "Ah. Ooh! Ah! Ooooh! It's broken! Send for the vet! Hello, Darren. She's broken my leg."

"He's coming —"

"The vet?"

" – the squares should keep him busy. We must check the king. I'm worried that the clod of grass may have slipped in the rain."

"Nobody would notice."

"Willoughby Chough is searching," said Darren. "*He* would notice."

"We'd better not all go," said George.

"I think we *should* all go," said Frisby. "It'll look odd if we don't."

"Let's all go," suggested George.

Darren hurried, wending in the sandy passageways.

"Old Darren takes this seriously," said George.

"Surely you do?" cried Frisby.

"Oh. Well. I suppose… But who wants to be serious?"

"George, you idiot, we are being followed by that horrid little man because he wants to steal an archaeological treasure! And!" Frisby thumped George with her knuckles. "We are being haunted! Or has that slipped your mind!"

"I was thinking about that," murmured George, rubbing his new bruise. "The *Field and Hedgerow* is published in Norwich. If we phone them they may send a copy with the rest of the story. Mind your feet on those roots."

"George?" Frisby looked up at him. "You do have a brain! I must tell Mother. And your dad'll be pleased."

"Probably," sighed George. "Any sign of Chuff-chuff?"

He ran suddenly, up the slope of a dune. Frisby ran after him.

"I see sand flying," announced George, "as the grave robber seeks the treasure!"

"You don't!"

"He must have found Darren's sticks and string by now."

Then they dashed, catching up with Darren, panting in the rain, for it was exhausting dodging through the dunes, thick wet sand sliding underfoot.

"Are we nearly there?" gasped Frisby.

"It's difficult to be sure." Darren looked back, though there was nothing to see but walls of sand. "No chance of him following? I'm looking for the ridge of fallen turf," he said. "I could tell better from the beach. These dunes are all the same."

"You're awfully wet," commented Frisby, frowning at Darren's jumper.

"The sun was shining when I came out this morning."

George pointed. "There it is. One ridge —"

"Stay back!" said Darren. "Footprints. The clod's still in place."

"You said not to move," protested George.

"Let's walk on, then turn back —"

"I thought we were going to make sure?" said Frisby. "I couldn't bear it if we were wrong."

"We weren't wrong," answered Darren. "You saw the crown, didn't you? You saw the jewels set in the gold. George?"

"Yeh," said George, staring at the earthen wall. "I'm sure. I just can't believe it. OK, Darren, no footprints near the king. Onward!"

Then: "Far enough! Back we go! Plenty of noise! Scare 'im off!"

So they trod the beach, salt seaweed flavouring the air, wavelets rushing to inspect their feet, inquisitive as puppies. Gulls flapped in leisurely flight away from their voices. George sped pebbles skipping on the shoulders of the water, slithering eventually, under the water's skin; while rain sighed; while Frisby applauded George's stones; while she searched the hazy distance...

"The mini's moving!"

"Victory!"

Darren ran. He disappeared among the dunes.

"You don't think Mr Chough's found the skull!" gasped Frisby.

"Come on!" said George. "Darren!"

"Here!" Darren was gazing around the real site of the skull and helmet. "Undisturbed."

He shivered.

"Come on!" cried George. And Frisby ran with Darren to the string squares.

"He's been digging!" said George gleefully. "Let's confuse him even more!" And with Frisby's help he moved the squares and dug again, laughing; Frisby watching Darren.

His lips moved as he panted; skin soft and white, like dough.

"We'd better get home," said Frisby firmly, and Darren followed her, George brushing sand from his hands, jolly as a donkey.

They cycled, then stopped at their usual parting place.

"You're coming for lunch!" said George. "Angel insists!"

Darren shook his head. Spikes of hair had risen from his rain-smooth head. He shrugged in his jumper. "Have to change."

"We'll wait."

"No," said Darren. "No. Don't wait. I'm a bit shivery. I think it's flu."

"A touch of plague," said George.

"A touch of plague," sighed Darren.

Chapter 19

"You shouldn't have left him!" said Mother.

"He was putting himself to bed, Angel."

"I'll serve the soup," said Frisby. "Three or four?"

"George has gone to the office," said Mother. "The greenhouse was too wet to take putty." So Frisby served three soups, and began to tell Mother – without giving away Darren's secrets – their adventure at the museum. But the doorbell rang.

"Who can that be!" sighed Mother.

"I'll go!" said Frisby, and she ran through the hall and opened the front door; to the rain; and the fat shape of Willoughby Chough.

"Oh!"

His feet wiped themselves on the doormat.

"Yes?" Frisby stood crucified between the door and the doorframe, her heart above her first spoonfuls of soup.

Willoughby Chough's mouth smiled. "I'd like to speak to your father. Frisby?"

"He's married to someone else," said Frisby.

"Married? Oh. I see." The mouth widened. "Your mother? This is most important —"

"She's busy. We're having our lunch —"

"Who is it?" Mother appeared in the hall.

Frisby looked round, relaxing her grip on the

door and indignation boiled when Willoughby Chough pushed in, saying loudly, "How important! A major find! I must talk to your children, Mrs...? This could be the saving of my museum..."

Willoughby Chough's suit hung dark with water. Sand clung to his sleeves and trouser legs. His left shoe had split across – with kneeling, thought Frisby, while trying to steal the king. Rain shone on his scalp.

Mother's glance went down him. She stepped back.

"George!"

"This is very important. Please. It could be the saving —"

"Hello?" said George. "So you followed us."

"Followed you!" cried Mother. "Was it you who frightened my daughter yesterday?"

"No. No! I didn't frighten anyone. I am —"

"You pushed past me!"

"How dare you come into my house!"

"This is very —"

"George, phone the police. Tell them that a tramp —"

"I'm not a —"

"I'll phone!" cried Frisby.

"No, no, no, no!" The man's feet slapped past Frisby. He turned on the doormat, eyes bright with anger, a smile gaping. "It's very important! Please! I am —"

Frisby shut the door on him.

"A tramp!" gasped Mother. "What a nerve! Oh, I'm shaking. I think you should tell the police anyway, George. He was soaked."

"Didn't have time to put his coat on," grinned George. "Don't worry Angel. That was Willoughby Chough. He wrote the story of Samuel Bath."

"What? Oh!"

"In Dad's magazine."

"You mean he's not a tramp?"

"He's been out in the rain all morning."

"Oh, you might have said!"

"You didn't give me the chance."

"I'm glad you threw him out!" cried Frisby. "Little beast! Greedy beast!"

"I'm going to eat my soup," said George.

"But what does he want!" Mother sat at the butcher's table. "Should we let him in? Oh." Mother smiled at Frisby, relief in the smile, and a little embarrassment.

George grinned over his soup. They laughed. Until the doorbell rang again.

Mother stared at George. She said, "I'll go. Now that I know he's not a tramp."

"I'll protect you," said George.

"I'm coming!" growled Frisby, just daring Willoughby Chough – in her mind – to try pushing past her again!

So they opened the door and filled the doorway.

"Your children —" announced Willoughby Chough.

"Children!" said George.

" – wanted to know about Samuel Bath. And the doctor's boy – is he here? You did want to

103

know what happened?"

"You really wrote the article?"

"Yes." Wipe, wipe went Willoughby Chough's feet.

"You may come in," said Mother, "if I can be sure there will be no more raised voices."

"You are quite right Mrs...?"

"Gray." Mother stood aside. George and Frisby stepped back. Willoughby Chough came into the house, shoes wet on the carpet; into the lounge.

"Frisby," said Mother. "Turn off the gas rings, darling." Frisby went, hearing Mother say, "Frisby's my daughter. She has my first husband's name. Frisby Allen. George..."

Frisby turned off the gas and finished her soup. She wanted Willoughby Chough out of her house. She wanted her lunch; after such a long wet morning her stomach sat flat with emptiness – though the soup helped.

She wanted to know the end of the tale of Samuel Bath, and she was determined that Willoughby Chough would learn nothing more about the king or the murderer's skull and helmet.

She returned to the lounge, lips firm over her teeth. Why, this horrid little man had followed them to the beach, then followed them home!

" – at school with my husband?" Mother was saying.

"Oh! I didn't know him! Part of a different crowd." His smile turned on Frisby. "Oh, yes. Hello again. Such a pretty child. Tell me where you found the bones." His eyes glittered. His scalp shone wet. His suit sank shapeless with water.

Frisby relaxed her lips into a smile. "Why did you follow us to the beach?"

"Oh, I didn't!" Fat fists closed. "I wouldn't! Really. I wouldn't."

"We saw your orange mini," said George.

"Were you following my ... children?" Mother leaned on the word 'children'.

"Mrs Gray, I would not contemplate... Why, what reason...?"

"You were shouting about something being important."

"I wanted to tell them about Samuel Bath."

"So you *were* following us! How horrid!"

"I didn't say —"

"Tell us about Samuel Bath," said Mother. "Before you leave."

"Why..." Willoughby Chough wiped water from his forehead, leaving his glitter of eyes sliding under his eyelids. His cheeks tugged his mouth into a smile. "Of course. Samuel Bath..."

"He saw a rat," Mother reminded him, "and the rectory smells of carrion. He rides to the place where he found the buckle. Then he feels someone staring at his back."

"He thought the rat was a warning," said Frisby.

"Yes. Yes, a warning. It's a long time since I wrote..." the eyes slid.

"Well, you'd better go." Mother stood suddenly. "After all, that's what you came for – to tell the *children* the story —"

"Please, Mrs Gray. I will remember. Let me gather my thoughts. My goodness. So hasty —"

"*We are in the middle of lunch!*"

"Of course you are! You did say. Well. Samuel Bath. On his mare. Well." His hands clung to his fat knees, rubbing grains of sand. "I don't recall how Samuel Bath was haunted ... but ... I would need a pen..."

George found him pen and paper. "There was plague, you know," said Willoughby Chough. "A sprinkling. Some dying, some not. Samuel Bath maintaining his duties. Visiting the sick. Spreading it, no doubt..."

His head bent to the paper.

The pen-tip circled, not writing.

Then he wrote, with many pauses, Frisby longing for lunch, curious to see Willoughby Chough's words.

Eventually, he handed the paper to Mother.

Mother gazed at it, hesitating, and a smile sat smug on the man's face.

"Shall I read it for you?" he simpered, then reddened, as Mother's school-teacher glance knocked his head back.

"I'm quite capable, thank you, of reading fourteenth century English. It is fourteenth century?"

"Yes."

"Octosyllabic couplet?"

Frisby smiled and George grinned.

"Well, yes —"

"Where did it come from?"

"Samuel Bath found it, researching. I have an interest in these things. I memorized it."

"So I see."

Mother read slowly, trying to put meaning into the strange words.

"Death he swims on the waves, In likeness of a cloud that rains, And pours sleep upon our land, Like seed cast from a skilful hand.

"Only the bones of Aethelhere, From Winwaed carried on his bier, Untouched in a pit doth lie – do lie – And thus protect those who cry For fear the pestilence does come.

"But should his bones be disturbed, Or sword or whetstone moved, The plague shall smite again the strand, Until the..." Mother frowned.

"Thief," said Willoughby Chough. "Robber."

"Thank you. Until the thief the part put in the ground Or forfeit life quite easily."

Mother smiled, solemn-eyed at the little man, and he inclined his head. "An educated lady."

"May I see?" cried Frisby, and George, who had scowled down at the page as Mother read, sat close. Frisby gasped. "Cripes!" she said.

Deth he swimmunde on the wawes,
En liknesse of a cloude that Reyns,
And poureth Slep upon owr land,
Lyke seed caste from a skilful hand.
Onely the bones of Aethelhere,
From Winwaed caried on his ber,
Vntouched In a pet doth lye,
And thus protecten those who cri
For ferde the Pestilence doth com.

107

But sholde his bones disturbèd be,
Or sworde or whetstone movede be,
The Plague schal smite agen the stronde,
Vntil the peleris part engrounde
Or forfeit lif al esely.

"How can you make sense of that!" cried Frisby.

"It's not difficult," said Mother, "once you understand the spelling."

"But what does it mean?" groaned George.

"Let me see it." Mother took the poem and read quietly.

"The first three lines," she said slowly, "refer, I think, to the coming of the Black Death, which is said to have rolled across Europe in the form of a visible cloud of bad air —"

"Quite right! Quite right!"

" – and the next part says that only the bones of Aethelhere protect us from the pestilence – the plague. But who Aethelhere was —"

"A king!" cried Willoughby Chough. "The whetstone —" His finger attacked the page. " – is a symbol of kingship. He was killed at the battle of Winwaed. You've heard of Sutton Hoo?"

"Of course," said George.

"Sutton Hoo?" said Frisby.

"Where they dug up a ship, Frizzy. Dug it out of the ground. Treasure!"

"We found its impression," corrected Willoughby Chough.

"We?" asked Mother. "You were involved?"

"Well, it's not far to Suffolk. I wasn't actually helping, but I took photographs. They knew who

I was —"

"How can you find an impression?" asked Frisby. "And why was a ship buried on land?"

"The timbers rotted away and their image was left in the ground. The ship was buried as a tomb for a king —"

"Aethelhere," said Mother.

"Aethelhere," agreed Willoughby Chough, "but he wasn't in it. There never was a body in the ship."

"So," said Mother, staring at the poem, "he was buried somewhere – on the coast? – to protect us from the Black Death."

"Aethelhere lived in the sixth century," said Willoughby Chough. "The plague came again and again. The worst visitation was 1348."

"Someone must have disturbed the king then," suggested Frisby. "Letting the plague in."

"That," said Mother, "we'll never know. But from the story, we can assume that Samuel Bath found the king's body and didn't realize. He picked up the buckle – and if you can believe it – caused a small epidemic —"

"Oh, no," said Frisby. "Samuel Bath found the body a hundred yards inland. The king is actually —" She gasped as George's foot struck her shin.

"What's that?" snapped Willoughby Chough.

His fat hand leapt on to Frisby's wrist. "Then you do know!" he hissed. "You do know, child! *You have found the bones of Aethelhere!*"

Chapter 20

Willoughby Chough's fingers clung wet on Frisby's skin.

"Let go!" She jerked free and rubbed her wrist dry. "Don't touch me!" she gasped, and was dismayed to feel tears brimming.

She ran to the kitchen. She dashed water from the tap onto her eyes and sat at the butcher's table gasping into a towel.

Voices moved through the hall, Willoughby Chough's urgent, Mother's regal, and George's casual. "Let me throw him down the step, Angel."

Then the front door banged, and George and Mother warmed the kitchen.

"Not your fault, Frizzy," announced George. "You always had a mouth like Paddington tube." But his look was gentle and Frisby's fist relaxed.

Mother lit the gas, and stirred pots.

Frisby ate another plate of tongue-burning soup; then potatoes and boiled sausages which sat excellent in her stomach until she remembered she was vegetarian.

"What's he doing?" she asked. "The little beast."

"I really don't want you to be rude," said Mother.

"Even if he is a little beast," said George. "I

110

should think – anyone want tea?" He answered nods by grabbing the kettle and battering water into it. "I should think he's dashed home for his wellies, and at this minute is parking the mini at the bridge, and by the time the kettle boils he'll be shoulder deep inside our string squares."

"You don't suppose he'll find the king?" Frisby found Mother staring at her. "What?" asked Frisby.

"I think," said Mother, "I should be told. That's twice you've said —"

"Oh!"

"Cough up, Frizzy," said George. "It's only fair. Angel hasn't poked her nose in at all – and she has helped..." *Clatter* went cups in George's grasp.

So Frisby told Mother of Darren's bronze strip, and the child-sized bone, and horror at touching a skull; then again about the ghosts running on the beach, and gold in the naked face of the land.

"Gold!" said Mother. "Thank you, George. Milk."

"I thought it was a wet stone. Darren spotted it was gold. A ring on a skeleton's finger!"

"You really have found a body!"

"Two," said George. "The man in the helmet and the skeleton with the ring. Three, if the little girl is buried with the man in the helmet, as the first small bone suggests. Darren is sure it belonged to a child."

"But is he sure..." Mother's cheeks paled under her sugar skin. "Is he sure they are not recent bodies? I mean —"

"Oh, Mum! Listen! The skull was exactly where Darren found the helmet. He says the helmet is 1349. *That* is the murderer! He says the first bone he found is a child's finger – a..."

"Phalanx," said George.

"And the king's body is miles away under layers of soil. It's simply been exposed by the sea..." Frisby frowned.

"What is it?" asked Mother.

"Of course. I was trying to remember something Darren said. At that part of the beach the sea takes away a little bit of land every year. Remember, George? He said where the murderer is, the beach stays more or less the same because of rock."

"So?"

"So, Georgie Porgie," said Frisby thoughtfully, "where the king is, the sea has eaten away a hundred metres – yards – of land since 1770; and the buckle Samuel Bath found was from our skeleton. Was it or wasn't it?"

"Wasn't it!" gasped George. "Brilliant, Frizzy!"

"Well," said Mother, "you've found the body Samuel Bath found. But what makes you think he's a king? A gold ring is not —"

"Not the ring, Mum! Not the ring... A crown!" whispered Frisby, and Mother's fingers tightened round her cup.

"A crown, Mum. One little spire of it. But it's all there! Solid gold, with a great ruby, and emeralds bright as moss. Oh, Mum! It was so beautiful! We were scared. We covered it again with grass."

"And it had the gold buckle," George reminded them, "until Samuel Bath took it."

"How could you keep such a secret?" whispered Mother.

George offered Mother the biscuits.

"George don't be rotten!" cried Frisby. Mother gave George a look.

"You have to report it," said Mother.

"Come off it, Angel!" groaned George. "Stop behaving like Any Other Parent!"

"But you must! It's important – Oh. Is that what the little man was shouting about?"

"Darren let slip about the skeleton." George left the kitchen and returned with Willoughby Chough's poem. He sniffed. "You got anything on your foot, Frizzy?"

Frisby shook her head.

"Bit whiffy in the hall. Maybe our visitor trod on something. Angel, go through the poem again. I've got the first bit, where the plague comes in a cloud of bad air. Aethelhere is supposed to keep it out, but doesn't, so as Frizzy says, someone maybe disturbed his bones in 1348. What's the *stronde*?"

"The shore."

"Longman's Reach," said Frisby.

"This is the difficult part," said George. "I can't even read it aloud."

"It's phonetic. You read every letter. *Peleris part* is robber's part. That is, the part of the king that he steals. Until the robber's part *engrounde*. In the ground. Buried. So it says that if Aethelhere is disturbed, the plague will come again until the

113

stolen part is returned or the thief is dead. Bit gruesome."

Frisby went and stood close to her mother. "It's scary," she explained. "We might have taken the ring. Or the crown. But Darren wouldn't hear of it. Someone's going to have to take everything," she said loudly, "to save it from the sea."

Mother smiled. "I should think Aethelhere heard you," she said kindly.

But it *was* scary.

"You know what Darren's dad said, Frizzy. There's almost no plague left in the world. I don't suppose even Aethelhere can let in an epidemic that doesn't exist. He might as well threaten us with an invasion of Vikings. And tell me if I'm wrong, Angel, but doesn't the poem read as if the warning is against thieving – not erosion? There was no plague when the sea took his foot. And if some chaps actually rescue Aethelhere from getting washed away – I mean archaeologists – I hardly think —"

"But if it's true," said Frisby, "about the plague coming if something is taken, why did it appear in Nanton yesterday, during the day? We didn't find the king until the evening – hours later."

"Hum," said George. Mother fingered a biscuit.

Frisby remembered Darren pushing something into his anorak in George's bedroom. She had seen his glance slip away when George mentioned the buckle found by Samuel Bath. But what it

114

might mean…

"It means it's all rot," sighed George. "Talking of rot…" His nose wrinkled. "There's something in the air."

"You're right," said Mother. "Now that the cooking smell is gone —"

"It's strong!" cried Frisby. "Ooh! D'you think it's a warning?"

"It's a warning to look where you tread!"

"It's getting worse!" Mother hurried from her teacup and opened the back door. Rain swung like a beaded curtain. "It's windy."

She strode across the kitchen and opened the door to the hall.

She stepped through.

"Oh, my goodness!"

Cold air shouldered the door shut.

"Angel?" said George.

Frisby heaved her chair back.

In the hall, against the door panels, something scratched.

Chapter 21

Wednesday afternoon. The thing in the hall.

Something bumped the bottom of the door.

Frisby knew instantly that the bumping was Mother's heels – as if she had stepped away from something. And the scratching was her fingernails as she felt for the handle.

Frisby thrust out of her chair.

Fast though she rose, George – goofy George – was a blur in her eye.

He tore the door open before Frisby was clear of the table. Something bounced across the tiles and rolled out into the rain.

Frisby rushed to the hall, past Mother in the doorway, past George staring where Mother pointed.

A dead shirt clung to the phone table's leg.

Frisby stared at the shirt.

The silly idea that Mother was scared of George's laundry, made her frown. She retreated and held Mother's arm.

"What is it?"

George eased Mother into the kitchen.

Frisby followed. She reached behind her, feeling for the door handle. She turned her head. The spindle which once held the handle, stuck naked from a hole in the door's timber. She said, "George?"

"Are you all right, Angel?" asked George.

"My heart's beating rather fast."

"George!?" said Frisby.

Mother's fingers closed around her teacup. Her hands trembled. George sat, his palm on her wrists.

"Mum?" said Frisby.

Mother nodded and gulped tea. "It's all right, darling."

Frisby didn't know what was wrong, but she wanted to touch Mummy's brown curls. She wanted to rub away the paleness under the sugar-soft cheeks.

But George was with her. And that was good.

"Mum," she said.

Mother's glance rose from the cup. She panted, but a smile bloomed, and her back straightened. "I'm fine. Really." She fumbled a pat on George's hand. "Thank you, George."

"Right, Angel." George went into the hall. Frisby glanced out the open back door at the rain. Something round shone in the mud. She heard the phone *ting*. Her slippers pittered across the tiles. She stepped into the rain.

"What have you got?" said Mother.

Frisby presented Mother with the brass knob from the hall door.

Raindrops trickled on the yellow metal. Mud ran between Frisby's fingers. She remembered mud on her face in the woods. She said quietly, "George tore it off the door."

The phone *ting*ed again.

Mother stared at the door knob.

"He moved so fast," said Frisby. She looked at

117

George as he came in.

"They'll post a *Field and Hedgerow* today. You've to send a cheque or postal order. What happened to the handle?"

"You phoned the publisher?"

George nodded and lifted the door knob.

"You pulled it off," said Frisby, "when you went after Mum."

For a moment George gazed into the metal's shine. He breathed "Huh!" then busied himself at the door with a screwdriver, exploding little noises of amazement.

"But what happened?" demanded Frisby.

"Angel saw the rat —"

"A rat!"

"*The* rat," said Mother. "Could you make hot tea, dear?"

"What d'you mean – *the* rat? Mum —"

"*The* rat, Frisby! Don't be so slow! The rat Samuel Bath saw!"

"Wha-at?"

"Please put the kettle on. No. Wait a minute. Don't put the kettle on. The smell in here is dreadful. We'll go out —"

"Mum!"

"It decomposed on the carpet. Did you see the skeleton, George?"

"Handle's fixed. Yes, I saw it. You're still a bit grey, Angel. I think going out's a good idea. Bit of a shock."

"George! You saw it? What does it mean?"

"Rats were plague carriers," said Mother. "I expect it's a warning. The new *Field and*

Hedgerow may tell us."

They hurried upstairs.

"George thought the little girl was trying to warn us," called Frisby to her mother's room.

"I'm ready!" bellowed George.

"I wish I'd seen it," said Frisby.

Frisby stopped Mother and George at Mason's window. She decided what clothes she would buy if she had a million pounds. Then they went into the store, George lingering, looking back at the museum.

"Forget Willoughby Chough!" said Frisby. She swirled her clean red coat and marched him and Mother to the tearoom.

Where they talked – of course – about Samuel Bath. Samuel Bath awakening ghosts in 1770 by taking the buckle. Discussing what might have wakened them yesterday; Frisby remembering Darren's guilty look when George mentioned the buckle.

And George wondering what had started the plague in 1348.

"That we'll never know," said Mother treating her mouth to a cake. "It's instead of all the biscuits I didn't eat!" she protested.

"One little cake won't hurt, Mum." Frisby gazed out the tearoom window at the town.

"Plenty of girls in school not half as neat as you, Angel."

"Thank you, George."

Frisby watched a woman with a child step up to the museum door. The woman pushed the door but it stayed shut. The child was dragged towards the shops.

"Why is the museum shut?"

"Shouldn't be," said George. "But Darren sometimes finds it deserted during the day. Reckons Willie Chough goes researching or boozing or —"

"Now, George."

"Have one of these pink cakes, Angel, with the cream."

"I'm full, Mum," said Frisby. "Can I go and look at the clothes?"

"Yes. We'll come in a few minutes. Don't leave the store."

She strode along, Frisby, feeling very grown up, pleased that her coat was like new – except for a little grit among the button threads. She would clean that carefully with a nail brush.

A leather jacket kept her attention until she remembered she was vegetarian. Was wearing animals as bad as eating them?

She wanted to see the clothes in the window. She left the shop and gazed through people's reflections at elegant plastic ladies and children.

One reflection stopped beside her own. She tried to see the price on a pair of boots. Fingers rested on her arm.

She looked up into Willoughby Chough's smile. The fingers tightened.

"I saw you going into the store. I waited for you. Your brother is still inside. Looks after you, doesn't he?"

Frisby jerked free. She pushed through

passersby. The fingers closed hard on her elbow. She pulled, but Willoughby Chough clung. She twisted her arm, breaking his grip, and ran to the shop door. He was at her back. Customers leaving Mason's blocked the entrance.

The fingers fumbled at her coat. She ran along the pavement, but people slowed her; and Willoughby Chough, by walking quickly, by trotting a little, kept close, saying, "Frisby, I only want a word. I only want to talk to you!"

She ran down an alley beside the store. Her coat seemed absurd, flowing grandly as her knees rose in rhythm, running, past bins and cardboard boxes; past steam from fans in the wall; damp smells on this dull day.

Willoughby Chough came wobbling, breath already hauling through his smile.

Ahead, the alley turned a corner to the back of the store. Frisby had never been here. She could probably continue right round on to the main street.

The alley stopped. A high wall enclosed a turning place for vehicles.

MASON'S GOODS ENTRANCE said a sign.

The entrance was a large double door and someone had forgotten to lock it. Frisby pulled open one half and slipped through. Facing her was a fire door. A notice said EXIT ONLY. The door had no handle. She pushed, but it wouldn't move.

A staircase invited her up. Willoughby Chough's shoulder eased through the double door. "I only want...!"

Frisby clattered up the stairs.

Another fire door stayed shut. She ran as Willoughby Chough came slapping on the steps.

He caught her at the top.

A landing made of concrete. A wire-glassed window too dirty to signal through. A door with no handle.

Willoughby Chough came gasping, sweat on his temples, a grey suit tight around his fat.

"I only want to talk!" he panted.

He stood one step down. "Tell me where Aethelhere is. Tell me! My museum..." He leaned a palm on the wall. Frisby darted to pass him, but he caught her round the neck. His fingers tightened among her curls.

"You're hurting me!"

"Tell me where!"

"Let go!"

She screamed as pain burned her scalp. Willoughby Chough threw her against the wall. Sobs heaved at her lungs.

The man no longer pretended to smile. He walked towards her and raised his hand. "Tell me!"

Frisby caught the blow on her arm. "I'll get the police!"

A second blow hesitated.

His cheeks bunched.

His voice said, "I'm sorry!"

But his eyes said, *I could slit your throat.*

He crouched beside her. Frisby had never seen such horrid eyes.

"Aethelhere is no use to you! You must hand

him over to the authorities. I am the authority in this town! Please! You are only a little girl! This means so much —"

Frisby darted.

Round him. He didn't reach for her. His feet did not slap behind her on the stairs. When she got to the road she looked back along the alley. He was walking past the bins, striding with anger.

Frisby ran into the shop and found Mother and George.

"There you are," said Mother. "See anything you liked?"

Chapter 22

Wednesday evening. Mother's roses.

Frisby said nothing about Willoughby Chough.

Even when Mother knocked dust from her coat – dust off the landing wall – even then, Frisby said nothing.

At first, she didn't know why. Reasons came as she walked with Mum and George through the afternoon.

Why, the little man could lose his job. And what if the treasure *would* save the museum...

"You're very quiet, darling. Perhaps we should go home. My feet —"

"We could meet Dad coming from the office, Angel. It's almost closing time."

So they met Mother's George and he drove them home; out of the busy streets; through the quiet roads; past the parting place for people on bikes; past Mum's roses —

"Stop the car!" yelled Frisby, "Stop the car!" And the car jerked to a halt half-along the drive. Frisby leapt out.

Mother's roses.

Their bonnets no longer turned from the wind.

Instead their petals rocked on the lawn.

Pink silk smudges mingled with the soil, trodden down as feet had snapped stems. Heel marks crossed the grass to the front door, and hollyhocks sprawled from their trellis, a colourful wreckage on the doorstep.

Behind Frisby, the car doors shut. George and his father strode about, faces blank with shock, Mother's George stepping over the hollyhocks and finding the house door secure.

Frisby took Mother weeping into the kitchen.

The smell was gone. It was time to eat; but tea with sugar was best.

The car crept towards the Small Barn.

Mother and Frisby drank tea, while the two Georges remained outside.

A hand beckoned at the kitchen window. Frisby and Mother walked round the house and stood beneath the drab sky. Soil spread flat now, around neat rose stems. A spot of pink still nodded here and there; and the hollyhocks stood straight on the red wall of the house.

"I pruned the roses." Mother's George put his arm over her shoulders. "I'm afraid some of the hollyhocks will die. They're held up with string."

"Thank you," said Mother. "Thank you, George."

"What do we do now, Dad? About Willoughby Chough."

"Yes," said his father. "I suppose it was him."

"But why?" sighed Mummy. "I can imagine him damaging the garden in a rage after we threw him out the house – but to come back this afternoon —"

"I saw him again," mumbled Frisby.

Everything had changed.

Frisby saw the wheelbarrow stacked with broken flowers.

If she hadn't threatened Willoughby Chough with the police, his second blow would have struck. She touched her bruised arm. He would have beaten her until she talked; or until she couldn't talk. Her hands trembled.

"But you were with us..."

"She's shaking," George's father stared down on Frisby. "Inside, please! I want the whole story. George, would you empty the barrow and put it away? I think it's raining. There, there, Frisby. Have a good cry..."

"George, the knives and forks are left-handed."

"Sorry, Angel!"

"Potatoes are almost ready. Frisby, hands. Not here! Use the bathroom!"

"She's still upset," said father George.

"There are dishes in the sink from lunch. Off you go!"

"I found out something," he said.

Frisby stopped at the door. Mummy turned to look at her husband, and young George paused, arms crossed as he rearranged the cutlery.

Mother's face set firmly. "Wash," she ordered. Frisby went.

She returned and sat at the table. Mother put the last of the dishes in the drying rack. She drained the potatoes, and served the meal.

"I went to Norwich this morning – on my way to the office."

"Norwich?" said Mother.

"What you said about this house having been a rectory, and the child appearing here, looking for help. I did some research. I knew already, of course, that the house dates back to 1743. But it was built by…" He sliced his chop, and chewed.

"I know!" cried George. "Samuel Bath!"

His father nodded. "So the ghost child didn't know this house in her lifetime. I mean, that was obvious —"

"But it might have been church property in the fourteenth century," said Mother, "which was what I said, and —"

"No, no! I looked deeper, Angel. In the library. Records go right back to the Domesday Book."

"I've heard of that," said Frisby. "It's about sheep and land —"

"It was a giant tax assessment by William the Conqueror. It preceded the plague by about three hundred years, but —" He prodded the air with his fork. " – right here – this very spot – was inhabited by a villein – that's a chap with quite a bit of freedom – and d'you know his name? Longman. Does that mean something?" He smiled at Mother.

"Longman's Reach!" gasped George.

"I should think your murderer," said his father, "was a descendant. Don't you? Three hundred years later? There's even the mention of a Small Barn, though ours isn't that ancient."

"Part of the stables are," said Frisby. "In the greenhouse. You can see the dark old stone near the ground. Just before the little girl appeared I thought that maybe the murderer lived there – that the stables might have been cottages."

"She's right," said father George. "You could

be right, Frisby. Now you mention it, the Small Barn has old stone for foundations. Well! Aren't we finding out! Your ghost isn't haunting *us* – she's haunting her old home."

He ate, then said, "I don't know about this stench, though. D'you think that's the child?"

"We think it's a warning, Dad" said George. "But we don't know what about."

After George – or was it Mother? – had asked for the tenth time how yesterday's haunting was caused, Frisby went to her bedroom.

She pulled a fashion book from a cupboard, then found her drawing pad. She placed water-colour paints on the carpet by her bed. She leaned against the bed, the pad on her knee, and stared at the illustration of a nineteen-twenties flapper. She began to draw.

The flapper's hair lengthened on the page. The dress coarsened into a smock. The Charleston-dance pose became a stance of pain, the thrown hand a gesture of despair.

Frisby used her tongue to moisten a brush. She touched scarlet onto the smock. She printed the date she had seen the child, and pinned the drawing to the wall.

She went to bed.

All her drawings floated in the dark as she lay under the duvet.

She was terrified of Willoughby Chough; terrified of his determination. His eyes had shown Frisby that he cared nothing for the hurt he caused. She couldn't imagine Willoughby

Chough's thoughts.

Knock on her door.

"Yes?"

"Hello?"

Her George's head bobbed in. "You were a bit shocked. Don't tell your mother, but I brought you a drop of medicine."

"What is it?" Frisby sat up. Tears rolled on her face. She rubbed her pyjama sleeve across them.

"The water of life."

"What's the water of life?" She smiled into the gloom.

"Glenmorangie." A glass pressed into her palm. "Sip it."

"Thank you!"

Perfumed fire on her tongue.

"Oh, it's super!"

"Take your time."

"Do I have to clean my teeth again?"

"They'll be cleaner than ever after that."

"Thank you. I was crying."

"Shock," said father George again.

Frisby felt his kindly warmth filling the room. He moved, and she saw his tall shape against the window.

"We thought of prosecuting him." He turned. "But with no witnesses... Your word against his, sort of thing."

"I don't want to go to court."

"Oh. No. But I'll see the police tomorrow. They'll warn him off. Let him know they're onto him. The police are good at that."

He approached, and his hand took the glass.

"Frisby."

Hesitation in the darkness.

"Yes?"

"You're my girl, now, y'know. Your father…"

Frisby knelt on the bed. She reached up and he bent to her embrace. Sobs quickened her breath. She didn't know why she was crying…

"I do love you," she said.

His fingers patted her shoulder.

"Good girl."

Frisby clung to him, his jacket collar under her forearm, his sticky bristles holding her cheek.

He eased her down, and pulled the duvet over her mouth. Frisby lifted her chin.

He said, "Goodnight."

"Goodnight, my George," said Frisby.

She slept.

Chapter 23

Thursday morning. The buckle.

She slept until George came bellowing at her door.

In the kitchen she demolished Rice Krispies, George saying, "Hurry up, if you're coming! I want to see Darren's black boils!"

"George!" from Mummy.

"Is…?" Frisby thought of her George. She held Mother's gaze. She said deliberately, "Has my dad gone to the office?"

Mother's head tilted, and white teeth peeped out from a smile.

"Come on!" grinned George.

"Your dad," beamed Mother, "left an hour ago. May your mum toast you another slice of bread?"

"No thanks!" Frisby glanced at the toaster. Beside it, letters lay in a slither. "Has the post been? Did the *Field and Hedgerow* come?"

Mother threw a large envelope on to the butcher's table. Frisby read "Norwich" on the postmark. The envelope was open. She pulled out the magazine.

"Frizzy! Come on! We've all read it! Never mind drinking more orange juice. I'll tell you about it on the way!" George made a face as he backed out into the yard.

"But what did Samuel Bath see when he was

out on his horse?" She ran to the cupboard under the stairs. She staggered into her wellingtons.

"He saw the ghosts!" called Mother. "He was so frightened —"

Frisby pushed herself into Mother's cold raincoat. She buttoned it as she ran to the kitchen. " – that he decided to return the buckle to —"

"Frizzy, come on!" George whirring his bicycle.

"Oh, I'll have to go!"

"Tell Darren I hope he's feeling better. Oh, wait. Take this —"

"Frizzy!"

Frisby snatched a plastic tub from Mother. "Biscuits," said Mother. "To keep me from eating them —"

"Frizzy —!"

She fled into the yard. George was standing patiently between the two bicycles. "Got to look after you. Dad says —"

"Very funny!"

" – that is – my dad and your dad —"

They cycled around the house. " – that is – George Gray —"

Frisby looked at the few spots of pink still nodding in the garden.

" – says he feels we are a real family now. This business has brought us together."

Frisby glimpsed the larch stump at the other side of the house.

"What about Samuel Bath?" She tightened her lips to keep from shrieking with joy. Then she thought fiercely of Willoughby Chough. *Her dad would sort him!*

"Samuel Bath searched for days," said George, "to find the place he'd found the buckle – so he could return it. He was that scared! But he also did some research and came up with Willie Chough's poem in the church records. The poem, of course, told him that the buckle was causing the local outbreak of plague. But he couldn't find the exact spot. The ground had been very dry, remember, and with the rain swelling the cracks... And he kept seeing the spooks. So he's out looking, and old Longman is running around, and Samuel bolts. Or his horse does —"

His mare, thought Frisby.

" – with Samuel clinging to the reins. Onto the beach. Galloping towards the toll house. And the bally ghosts did their act – you know – the woman falling. And the horse threw him and scarpered. Here we are. Darren's mum is at the window. She must have stayed off work."

"Tell me the rest! Before she opens the door!"

"He hid among the dunes – but later thought that the place where he hid meant something, for all three spooks rose around him, and in panic he threw the buckle onto the sand and fled. He was killed later when the bridge collapsed. He didn't return the buckle to the right place, Frizzy, so he copped it. Splash! There's Mrs Wycroft. Oh, yes – interesting thing – he wrote the whole story down, but *being ashamed of his cupidity*, he hid the manuscript in his spinet. I suppose somebody else wrote about his death.

"And it was in the spinet that the writer of the old newspaper article found it —"

"Hello, Mrs Wycroft. How's Darren?"

" – then Willoughby Chough found the old newspaper and wrote the articles for the *Field and Hedgerow* – Hello, Mrs Wycroft. Is Darren any better? Mum sent him biscuits."

Frisby crept into Darren's bedroom. She felt the door should be marked with a skull and crossbones.

George strode to the bed.

Darren opened his eyes, green as seaweed. "Hello."

Frisby shivered in the cool air.

"Are you dying!" demanded George.

"Course not. It's only flu."

"Looks like plague to me."

"I've got a temperature."

"We've all got a temperature."

"A hundred and one," panted Darren.

"Do you want us to go?" asked Frisby. She didn't like this room, with junk enough to fill a shop, and Darren's photos stuck on the walls, showing dark corners of landscape.

"No, don't go. I have an idea. I feel light-headed. My hands are tingling." His palms splayed, like pink tissue paper. "My temperature. I may be extra sensitive. You know."

"Oh," said Frisby.

"Give me the helmet. On the chest-of-drawers."

Frisby stepped over books. She saw the strip of

134

helmet among the junk. The top drawer, just under her reaching hand, sat open. A glint of light drew Frisby's eye inside the drawer. She changed the direction of her hand. Without thinking she lifted out a golden badge; startlingly heavy, sun-bright and formed of many fine scrolls... She gaped.

"Come on, Frizzy," said George. She lifted the helmet, hiding the badge at her side. She threw the helmet onto the bed, then presented the gleaming scrolls to the daylight.

George's mouth opened. Darren's glance rose from the bronze. He said, "Ah."

"Ah!" cried Frisby. "Ah? Is that all you can say! D'you think we don't know what this is? It's Samuel Bath's buckle! George? Samuel Bath *died* because of this!" She threw the buckle at Darren and he clutched his chest. "Now *you've* got it!" she screamed.

Chapter 24

Thursday morning. The murderer speaks.

"Calm down, Frizzy," said George.

Darren rubbed his chest.

"Darren will tell us. It's only one of his secrets." George took the buckle from Darren's hand. He said, "Wow," quietly. "This really is something. Where —?"

"Were you going to keep it?" snapped Frisby. "You're as bad as Willoughby Chough!"

"No!" gasped Darren. Sweat glowed on his brow. His hair stood spiked, like a dark halo against the pillow. "Only for a day or two. It has to be catalogued. It has to fill its place in history. You understand? It wouldn't be complete if I kept it. It's part of everything that has happened over the last thousand years."

"But where did you get it!"

"Beside the helmet." Darren's palms enclosed the strip of bronze. "I found it along with the helmet. Tuesday morning... I felt someone watching as I picked it up..."

Frisby shrank against George. She stared at Darren's sweating face, hands praying around the bronze strip.

"Then *you* started it!" she whispered. "*You* took the buckle and disturbed the ghosts! *You* caused this outbreak of plague, and sent the ghosts chasing after me in the wood!"

She raised her fist —

Darren's hands smothered his face, then slid away leaving the bronze protecting his nose, the rotting edges curving above the slither of his eyes.

Frisby forgot her fear.

A voice, coarse in his throat, formed words that made Frisby frown and George lean over the bed.

"What's he saying!" whispered Frisby. "Is it the poem? Is he quoting?"

"It's not the poem."

The voice lightened. The words rang in a clear breath across the room, and the hair on Frisby's neck prickled, for they were not Darren's words, but memories plucked from the helmet.

And he said, "My Lord Gossand mocks me with the glorious name of Aethelhere —" George's hand crushed Frisby's shoulder. " – but he knows not the truth in the old wives' tales."

"Oh, George!"

"But I know. And searching, find. I wear the crown —"

"He took the crown!" gasped Frisby, and she stood, her skin rippling, listening to this voice from the past, realizing that Longman, the murderer, had let in the Great Pestilence by stealing the crown of Aethelhere...

" – but its beauty weighs cold in my heart, for in this year of our Lord thirteen hundred and forty-eight, Aethelhere fills the sky with death, and I weep not. Instead, my Lord Gossand gives me more rejoicing, for he summons me, knowing my love of gold and says, 'The cattle are dying.

The swine rot in their styes. The very rats shrivel in the wainscot; the servants suppurate and bleed and I cast them and their stench out!'"

"The smell!" gasped Frisby.

"'I will not die because a scullion breathes poison, so thou shalt slay them, and no man shall turn his hand against thee, for thou art mine, and each time thy sword drinks, more gold shall I pour into thy purse!'

"And I rejoice, and day by day my sword sups the red wine of profit.

"And the year passes.

"My God, how I long for thee! Oh, the hollowness of greed! Do I continue craving gold until my last lit candle?

"But my heart is lost, and through this land I stride, a slayer of innocents, until... Oh! my child... My own sweet babe, I see thy corrupt flesh and condemn thee. And thou knowest my intent and flee, and thy mother fingers my garments, mumbling and weeping. And on the eleventh day I seek thee in thy hiding place among the dunes. On your weak limbs do ye run, but thy mother's fear guides me. She falls, and then thou must flee seeking sanctuary in the church.

"But God's servants bolt His door against thee, and thy pleading hands ye turn to me, thy father.

"And though my heart swells, I cleave thee in twain.

"Then I know what I have done.

"I gather up thy flesh, and in your hiding place among the dunes, I bury thee deep. I return the crown to Aethelhere, and leave him so no man will discover him again.

"So I return to thee, my daughter, and calling on God's mercy, I fall upon my sword."

Chapter 25

Thursday morning. Longman's Reach.

George and Frisby cycled, leaning on the wind.

Rain drove against them.

They rode, standing on their pedals.

The shore came roaring to meet them.

They stood on the bridge at the toll house pub, holding their bicycles, the sea beckoning all along the wandering sand. They gazed at the orange mini, parked on the bridge beside them, its metal skin rolling with raindrops; George, more serious than Frisby had ever seen him, pushed his finger along the mini's roof. "Good thing we came. If a wave washes away the clod of grass, Chuff-chuff could find the skeleton."

Frisby leaned her cycle on the bridge wall and stood close to George. She shivered, not from cold – though the rain lay cool on her face – but at Darren green-eyed behind the helmet, *tasting* the murderer's past.

"Georgie Porgie?" she whispered.

His arm slid around her shoulders.

"Yes."

"That murderer found the king."

"He put the crown back," sighed George, "after a year of killing."

A wave rose in the sea, like a mile-long monster.

"You were right!" said George, above the

noise. "Darren started it all, by taking the buckle. But he wasn't to know..."

"Will he die?"

"It's only flu, Frizzy. And he didn't steal the buckle from Aethelhere. He took it from where Samuel Bath dropped it on the sand. Though that was disturbance enough to set things moving. I wonder how often it was exposed over the centuries. This place has always been haunted. Into the sand it went, right where the little girl is buried. And her father. Look at that sea. It's pounding up past the high tide mark. I hope Willie Chough can swim!"

George ran, his feet gouging the sand.

Frisby ran, and the sea heaved a wave that made her look up. The wave dropped, smashing the sand, spitting on her.

"Get among the dunes!" yelled George. She followed. Sand leapt from his heels onto Mother's coat. She saw Willoughby Chough's footprints ahead of George, and *crash!* said a wave on the lowest dunes, *crash!* and spray pattered down, froth on George's hair.

At the string squares sea water drained from the digging.

"He knows there's nothing there!" shouted George. He ran on. *Crash!* Down came the sea. Frisby shrieked; wet they ran on, *crash!* and water rushed green towards her feet and slid away; but George splashed ahead, winding in the roofless passageways. Past the site of the murderer and his girl, feet pounding the slipping sand; to do what? thought Frisby. *To stop*

Willoughby Chough? Float him over to Holland?
    CRASH!
    George cried out, and Frisby screamed as water dropped on them, heavy like a wet pillow swung by a giant, breaking on her head, bursting on her shoulder, scalding cold down her neck and under her clothes.

    But they plunged on, sea frothing in Willoughby Chough's footprints. Sand in Frisby's teeth, raised by desperate waves, and she panted after George, hoping he would know what to do if Willoughby Chough had found the bones of Aethelhere.

    The sea raged.

    A wooden crate balanced high on a dune. Rags of seaweed wriggled in retreating water. *Crash!* screamed the sea. Waves dropped around them and they fell, tumbling in the water's dragging bulk; kneeling, running again, George leading on, heroic in his silence.

    They found him.

    Willoughby Chough.

    His back to them, kneeling in his wet grey suit. And Frisby saw the bones of the king's leg, scoured free by the sea. George shouted.

    Not a word, but indignation. Not the man's name, but righteous anger, and he shouted again through the fury of water, and Willoughby Chough looked over his shoulder; and his eye shone as though his sword had drunk of blood. He turned away, then stood clumsily, and faced George, the crown of Aethelhere in his hand.

    "Put it back!" cried George.

"It's mine!" shrieked Willoughby Chough.

"It's the crown of Aethelhere!"

"It is the crown of Willoughby Chough! Aethelhere gave it to me! Beckoning with his finger, his ring gleaming. You can't have it —"

"I don't want it!" yelled George.

" – it's mine! For my museum! For *me!*"

"Put it back!" George stepped closer.

"No!" The crown in Willoughby Chough's hand rose in a curve of light and the little man took a stride forward. The light struck George's forehead and Frisby gasped.

George fell. A wave roared clawing over the dunes.

George sprawled, groaning. Willoughby Chough ran into the wave, the crown glorious in his grasp.

Frisby dropped across George, and water beat her flat, like a great stone that broke as it struck, pressing the breath from her in a cry that only she heard; and she would have cried again, but water swelled, drowning her, drowning George whose arms floated; and the water rushed away, rolling her off George, and she clung to his clothing, and he drifted as the water fled, and lay limp as a sack; the sea sighed, and left them, Frisby gasping, weeping at water running from George's mouth.

Her bones were rubber. She shrieked at her body to move. Another wave would finish them. She heaved George face down. She sent her weight onto his back. More water ran from his mouth and nose. Again she thrust down and he coughed and she howled in his ear to *get up! get up!* The sea came again; over the dunes; sweeping sand as it came; ripping off grass, dropping.

George was up, his fingers tight on Frisby's wrist, and they staggered in the sliding sand to the king's bones, over the king and sprawled away onto the land, under the wires of the fence.

The sea dropped, green fury, roaring in failure along the beach.

"Mr Chough!" panted Frisby. "George!" Another wave broke on the dunes, but its energy was less, and Frisby clung to George as he jumped down again to the sand.

He steadied her. "You stay here."

"No!"

"Come on, then."

George, shocked white, glanced at the wall of land. "Old Aethelhere's leg's gone. Need to call in the archaeologists now."

"Hurry!" She clung to George, gaping at foam and water running from the dune tops, small rivers returning to the sea. Another wave crashed, but George only crouched as it pattered around them, and Frisby bit on a cry.

Then George ran, dragging her, around dunes, closer to the shore. "*I don't see him!*" then hauling her towards the land again as the sea rolled in.

"We must find him!" screamed Frisby, and they waited until the next wave struck, then ran in its rushing wake, George's fingers bound like iron on Frisby's wrist; then again they retreated, and water fell, turning them like toys, drowning

Frisby until the wave slid, vanishing. Salt water in her throat and nose, coughing; George coughing, still iron-clasped around her arm.

George dragged her onto the land and pushed her through the fence where oats, flat-blasted by the sea made a slippy walking place. Then they stepped among standing oats, breaking a safe path, following the shore; stopping, waist deep amid nodding seedheads; while the sea crashed all along the land, exploding house-high, spray stinging Frisby's cheeks as if to say, *I can still reach you.*

Frisby followed George through the field, to the bridge at the toll house pub.

They avoided looking at the mini.

They pedalled shakily, then fiercely, home.

They wept in the kitchen; George, an elbow on the butcher's table, one hand supporting his cheek, letting tears run without shame. Frisby crouched in a chair wide-eyed and sobbing, watching Mother run in efficient panic, bringing towels and blankets, patting a towel on Frisby's face, dabbing George's eyes as if he were her baby.

Then she poured Glenmorangie and the whisky burned softly down Frisby's throat and spread heat through her body.

Coffee followed, with bread and butter and slices of the ham.

Then, as Mother took Frisby to the shower to wash away the salt, to wash away the fear, the phone said *ting!* and they paused on the stair, gazing down on George, blanket-wrapped, dripping, face into the phone's red plastic.

Chapter 26

The following Monday.

"Then George phoned the coastguard," said Frisby.

In the lounge, reporters bowed to their note pads.

Mother moved through a haze of sunlight, coffee glittering on a tray.

"Thank you," arose around the room.

"Move closer, Darren," said a girl with a camera. *Blot!* said the camera and green fish swam in Frisby's eyes.

"So what happened next?" asked a man. "Who found Willoughby Chough?"

"He was all dead," sighed George.

"Darren found him," said Frisby. She touched Darren's hand. "You must have been on the beach while we were crossing the field."

"But I thought you were ill?" A woman stared over reading spectacles at Darren's pale face.

"Yes —"

"... out of his sick-bed..." she muttered into her pad.

"After they left my house..." Darren looked at George, then smiled his bent smile at Frisby and she nodded encouragingly.

"After they left ... I lay in bed. The helmet had slipped onto my cheek. Different images came. Of the sea tearing at the land. People among the dunes. I knew the treasure was in danger. I sneaked past my mother, and cycled. I wasn't very steady. I fell off my bike on the sand, and ran. Staggered really.

"The wind had died. I found Willoughby Chough standing against a dune, staring at me – I thought – with his arms out as if appealing for help. But he didn't move. And in his fist..." Darren's voice had faded to a whisper. " – in his tight little fist..."

Pencils stirred over pads.

"Get on!" hissed Frisby.

Darren gazed at her.

"... the crown of Aethelhere."

Sudden breathing in the lounge.

"I crouched against another dune," said Darren, "just looking. I was pretty ill. The police came eventually. I remember a coastguard launch cruising near the shore. That was last Thursday."

Silence wandered in the sunlight.

George touched the bruise on his forehead.

A match scraped the silence.

Someone said, "Well..."

"We're going shopping," announced Frisby, and Mother stood up.

"Spending your share of the treasure?"

"The children..." said Mother, "... ah ... the youngsters will be awarded something. No, we don't know how much yet. It will take months to assess. Quite a large payment probably. Especially when a hoard of gold was found with the child's bones." Mother gathered cups and cigarette ends. "Blood money."

"How does your stepfather feel about your new wealth?" The woman with the spectacles stared at Frisby.

"My dad," said Frisby, "feels fine. Thank you. You will remember to return the drawing of the little girl when you've printed it in your newspaper?"

The woman nodded.

"Thank you," said Mother. "Goodbye." She smiled everyone towards the hall.

"One last question. Have there been any more plague victims. Darren?"

"Three altogether. Seems they knew someone who had been hitch-hiking in the middle east. The authorities are still on the alert, but..."

"Will you do any more treasure hunting?"

"You have the whole story," said Mother. "Goodbye. Goodbye."

She shut the front door.

"Are we going shopping now, Mum? I wish it wasn't so hot! I could wear my good coat!"

"Come on!" groaned George. He grabbed Darren, and they tumbled noisily out through the kitchen.

"I'm glad that's over," said Mother. "We will now have a very pleasant day shopping. And a meal out. Just the two of us."

"Where will we eat?" asked Frisby.

"I don't mind," said Mother. "Somewhere really nice. After all," she smiled, "you're paying."

THE PLACE BETWEEN

Hugh Scott

"Don't you know The Place Between? That's what I call it... In the darkness, there is somewhere else that comes between me and this world."

Waking late at night, Stella discovers her friend Daniel at her door, terrified, pleading to be let in. The fearful scratching sounds that follow give credence to his tale of haunted woods and creepy scrabbling twigs. Events quickly become even more sinister and dramatic, until there seems to be only one conclusion: some weird supernatural power is at work. A power that threatens to consume anyone in its path...

"Hugh Scott is a master of the genre."
The Sunday Telegraph

SHADOW UNDER THE SEA

Geoffrey Trease

A hand grabbed the collar of her denim jacket and jerked her savagely to her feet. She found herself looking down the barrel of Shulgin's gun.

In the new Russia of *glasnost* and *perestroika*, making friends can be surprisingly easy – as Kate discovers when she meets Stepan and Marina. But the bad old days aren't over yet – not while the sinister Comrade Shulgin is alive and plotting…

"Crime and archaeological discovery and teenage romance are deftly interwoven in this beautifully paced, engrossing story."
The Times Educational Supplement

A GHOST WAITING

Hugh Scott

"The pale thing rose into the torchlight. It flapped towards Andrew and Rosie..."

It begins for Rosie and Andrew one stormy afternoon, about a year after the death of their brother James, in the gloom of their father's churchyard. A white rushing thing, a split gravestone, a sense of something lurking in the shadows... It isn't really the start, though, but the final chapter of a story begun centuries before by a scheming cleric – and continued now by a reckless teenage boy. And before the terror ends, someone must perish...

"Horror and good writing don't often go hand in hand – Scott is a master of the genre." *The Sunday Telegraph*

WHY WEEPS THE BROGAN?

Hugh Scott

WED. 4 YEARS 81 DAYS FROM HOSTILITIES ...
so reads the date on the clock in central
hall. For Saxon and Gilbert, though, it's
just another day in their ritualized indoor
existence. Saxon bakes, Gilbert brushes,
together they visit the Irradiated Food
Store, guarding against spiders. Among
the dusty display cases, however, a far
more disturbing creature moves... But
what *is* the Brogan? And why does it
weep?

"Deftly evoked, the narrative is cleverly
constructed, and there is no denying the
nightmarish power of the story. There is a
true shock ending." *The Listener*

"A very compelling and very interesting
book." *Jill Paton Walsh, The Times
Educational Supplement*

A Whitbread Novel award-winner
Shortlisted for the McVitie's Prize

A BOX OF TRICKS

Hugh Scott

"Simon Welkin! Come! We would converse with thee!"

Every summer, John and Maggie are packed off to stay with their Aunt Nell and Great-grandfather Harris in the country. But this year they get an explosive surprise, when Great-grandfather decides to waken the dead!

"Hugh Scott is at his best, stretching and exciting the imagination, producing glittering effects... Eerie and occasionally terrifying, beautifully evoking dark and light... The tension mounts to make the pulse race." *Susan Hill, The Sunday Times*

"Horror-hungry 10-year-olds will love it." *The Sunday Telegraph*

"A book which will be read time and again – a captivating ghost story which could well become a classic." *Time Out*

THE CAMERA OBSCURA

Hugh Scott

Spindletrim Tom's life at school is blighted by three bullies. His only refuge is Grandfather's antique shop, above which one day he discovers an amazing secret – a way of seeing into the past, present and future: the camera obscura. It's the start of some extraordinary events...

"The most intriguing and certainly the most excitingly written book I have read for a long time."
Mary Hoffman, The Sunday Telegraph

"Displays a Dahl-like exuberance and relish for the flesh and blood... An intriguing story." *School Librarian*

"It is full of fine lines and memorable images." *Jan Mark, The Times Educational Supplement*

CALABRIAN QUEST

Geoffrey Trease

Her heart nearly stopped… The figure was human – but the head upturned to meet her incredulous stare was the head of a wolf.

A fifth-century Roman christening spoon is the catalyst for this thrilling adventure which sees Max, a young American, travel to Italy with Andy, Karen and her cousin Julie on a quest for lost treasure. It's not long, though, before they encounter some sinister happenings and find themselves in conflict with the local Mafia…

"A gripping story of achaeological adventure… The tale rattles along, demonstrating an unputdownability as durable as [Geoffrey Trease] himself."
Mary Hoffman, The Sunday Telegraph

"From storytelling such as this, readers are infected with a love of books."
Jill Paton Walsh, The Times Educational Supplement

SOMETHING WATCHING

Hugh Scott

Beyond the table, something reared. Two tiny dots of light stared at Alice. The thing had grown. In its blackness she saw faint patterns of paw prints on sand...

Alice first sees the leopard-skin coat when her mother is clearing out the loft, ready for the family's move to an old castle – and it makes her shudder. Attached to the coat is a label insisting that it be burned, but without explanation. It soon becomes obvious, though, that something evil has been unleashed. Something monstrous. Something that means the family harm.

"A chilling tale in true gothic style, building to a spine-chilling climax." *The Times*

THE GARGOYLE

Hugh Scott

"No! No! No! You don't understand! The fear will kill you!"

On first sight, the new Scottish home of Professor Kent and his family seems quite idyllic. But there's a chill about the place that's not simply due to snow – an atmosphere of menace that young Marion, with her psychic powers, quickly senses. It seems to have something to do with the mysterious German and a boy called Callum who live in the nearby castle. Before long, Marion and her father find themselves in a tense battle of wits and wills – a life and death struggle that brings them face to face with the terrifying gargoyle...

"Followers of Hugh Scott will relish the mannered deliberation with which menace builds up in *The Gargoyle*."
The Independent

"The kind of book that once you start you've got to finish. You can't possibly put it down for another sitting. It moves at a pretty cracking pace."
BBC Radio's Treasure Islands

MORE WALKER PAPERBACKS
For You to Enjoy